BARAN'S FATE

LUMBERCATS VOLUME 3

SAMANTHA CONLEY

CHAPTER 1

The sun beat down on Lerna Porter's dark head, although it was the first week of March. What was wrong with this state? Was it close to hell? Sweat trickled down her back underneath her long-sleeved shirt. She wasn't prepared for the warm weather down here. Wiping the sweat threatening to drip into her eyes, she glanced up at the cloudless sky. Up in Chicago, the weather was frigid, and she hadn't thought to grab any lighter weight clothes. She dodged others on the sidewalk and envied their shorts and sandals. She stuck out like a sore thumb here and that worried her.

Lerna had spent almost all her cash on the bus ticket from Chicago to Dallas. The attendant at the bus station took pity on her when she had explained she was escaping her abusive boyfriend. She pulled her long brown hair off her nape and peered into the window to her left. A couple sat at a table eating ice cream. Now that was a good way to cool off.

She pushed open the glass door and let the cold air wash over her. She walked to the counter and looked over the multitude of flavors.

"Good afternoon. What can I get you?" A perky young girl asked from behind the counter.

"What would you recommend?"

"It's all delicious, but my favorite right now is the peaches and cream."

"I'll take a scoop of that and a water."

"Cone or cup?"

"Cone please."

"That'll be four seventy-nine," the girl said after she rang up my purchase.

Lerna pulled a five-dollar bill out of her pocket to pay and dropped her change in the tip jar sitting by the register.

"Thank you and come again," the girl stated as she moved to the next customer.

Lerna put the bottle of water in the pocket of her bag and took a small bite of her ice cream. The taste of peaches blasted across her tongue. She stepped into the crowd traveling on the sidewalk. The heat beat down, causing her ice cream to drip down the side of the cone. Lerna dipped her head to lick a drop off the side, and her attention caught on something on the other side of the street. Or someone. Her blood frozen in her veins. It couldn't be.

Lerna did a double take, and he was no longer there. She picked up her pace anyway. She weaved around a group of women milling around in front of one of the boutique windows. A gentleman stepped out of a doorway and bumped her elbow. Her ice cream fell to the concrete with a plop.

"I'm sorry. I didn't see you there," the man apologized. "Can I buy you another one?"

He lacked the accent she had heard the past few hours. He sounded as if he hailed from the north. She tensed when he placed a hand on her arm.

"It's alright. Thank you though. I'm in a hurry."

"Maybe I can take you out to dinner instead? I hate that I made you drop your treat."

"I'm only in town for a visit. Thank you, though." Lerna pulled her arm away and took a step away from him. A group of noisy teenagers jostled her, and he grabbed her wrist. He slid a business card into her hand.

"If you change your mind. Give me a call." He smiled, and a dimple appeared in his left cheek.

Lerna nodded with a smile and walked away. After a few feet, she glanced over her shoulder to find him standing in the middle of the sidewalk, staring at her retreating form. She shook off the sense of dread that had come over her. He was just a man. Not someone who was tracking her down.

Lerna's hotel was a couple of blocks up the street. She had scored a good deal, but it had cost the last of her cash. She needed to find a way to make some cash. Her eyes darted around, paranoia riding her hard. She felt eyes on her, but she couldn't pinpoint the source.

Lerna walked up to the hotel's door, and it slid open, bathing her in cool air. She kept her head down and made her way through the lobby to the elevators. As she stood waiting for the doors to open, a gentleman came up beside her. Lerna kept her gaze averted, but noticed the expensive navy suit covering his wiry frame. The brown loafers on his feet caught her attention. They were the same ones that her ex-boyfriend Angelo wore, the ones he bragged that cost more than she made in a week.

The doors opened, and she hesitated walking in. The man didn't have the same issue and entered.

"Going up?" he asked when she continued to stand there.

Lerna bit back her fear and entered the elevator. She pushed the button for the third floor. The one for the sixth was already lit up. She kept to the back corner of the metal box; her bag clutched in her arms, shielding her. When the door opened on her floor, she hurried out. The doors shut with a thud, and she turned to face the man, but no one was there.

"Get it together, Lerna," she mumbled to herself.

She pulled her keycard out of her pocket and slid it into the lock. The light turned from red to green and she opened the door. She wilted against the wall after she locked the door. The room was clean but sparse. She dropped her bag on the chair. She needed to call her sister, but she was desperate for a shower to wash away the sweat. How did people live with this heat in the spring?

After a brief cleanse, she pulled on a pair of soft lounge pants and a cropped pink shirt. Lerna fished the pay as you go phone from the bottom of her bag. Her sister, Veronica, was the one phone number she had memorized. It rang and went to voicemail. Lerna called her right back and Veronica answered.

"Hello?"

Lerna closed her eyes in relief at the sound of her sister's voice.

"Hey it's me," Lerna uttered.

"Oh, thank God. I was freaking out. Where the hell are you?"

"It may be safer if you don't know."

"Jesus, Lerna. What the hell is going on?"

She pictured Ronnie pacing back and forth in her office, heels clacking on the wood flooring.

"I can't tell you," she admitted. "It's safer that way."

"Some guy was here asking about you yesterday. It freaked me out."

"What did you tell him?"

"Not a damn thing. I had security escort him out. What kind of trouble are you in?" Ronnie begged.

"The kind that could get me killed."

"Oh, my God."

"I don't know what I'm doing, Ronnie," she confessed.

"This has to do with that guy you've been seeing, doesn't it? I knew there was something fishy about him."

"You were right. Is that what you want to hear?"

"No. What I want is you safe! Is he with you?"

"No."

"Is he what you're running from?"

"Yes."

"Oh, my God," she uttered.

"Would you please quit with that," Lerna snapped.

"Well, excuse me for not knowing what to say when my baby sister is in danger."

"I'm sorry." Lerna plopped down on the bed. "I'm freaking out!"

"Call the cops."

"I can't."

"Why not?"

"He said he had some of them in his pocket."

"In his pocket? Is he in the freaking mob?" Ronnie whisper yelled.

"The less you know, the better."

"What can I do?"

"I'm out of money. I can't use my credit or debit cards in case he has some way to trace them."

"I can't wire you money. They'll want identification, but I'll figure out a way to get you some."

"You're a lifesaver."

"Are you someplace safe?"

"I'm in a hotel room. I sweet-talked them into letting me pay cash for the night. I told them my wallet was stolen."

"Give me the address and I will have some food sent to you."

"What if they're monitoring you? They found out where you worked!"

"They could have found that on social media. I'm sure you told him that you have a sister."

"I did."

"Look, I'll have my assistant order it for you. Give me the address."

Lerna rattled off the address and room number.

"Texas, huh?"

"I figured it was far enough away, but it's freaking hot here."

"Do you want me to find a way to get you here?"

Here was Phoenix, Arizona.

"Not yet. I need to decide the next move."

"I think you need to call the cops and tell them everything."

"But what if it's the wrong cop? What if he runs to Angelo and tells him where I am?"

"Damn it," Ronnie huffed.

"I know. I ran before he could find me and now, I don't know what to do."

"Let me makes some calls. Jeff's brother is on the force here. Maybe he can be of some help."

Jeff was her boyfriend that she had met when she moved into her condo.

"Okay. I'll call you back tomorrow night."

"If I don't hear from you, I'm calling in the cavalry," Ronnie warned.

"Thanks, sis."

"You stay safe. I'll get you some money there tomorrow."

The phone disconnected, and Lerna stared at it. What she wouldn't give to be with her sister right now. Lerna flipped through the television channels until she heard a knock on the door. Her heart stopped for a second before resuming at a frantic pace.

"DoorDash," a deep voice called through the closed door.

"Just leave it by the door," Lerna called out.

"Yes, ma'am," he called out.

After a few minutes, Lerna crawled off the bed. She

looked out the peephole but didn't see anyone in the hallway. She flipped open the locks and pulled the door open. A brown paper bag sat on the ground along with a white Styrofoam cup. Lerna stooped to pick them up when a hand covered her mouth and shoved her back into the room.

"Hello, Princess."

CHAPTER 2

Baran Rhodes wiped the sweat off his brow. The east Texas sun beat down on him and his crew as they worked to clear the areas of the diseased pine trees. Chainsaws growled as his men worked. He walked over to his truck and grabbed the jug of water he had left there. The lukewarm water wet his parched throat and dampened his gray cotton shirt, and it dripped off his beard.

"Fuck, it's hot," Tarek Kirks griped as he walked up beside Baran. His navy t-shirt was drenched with sweat and his salt and pepper hair was plastered to his head.

"Gotta love Texas weather. It was in the fifties last week."

"I'd rather work in the cold," Tarek grunted.

"We're making steady progress." Baran nodded at the area. "Only a few more acres left of this area."

Tarek tossed his yellow hard hat, picked up his red jug from the bed of the truck, and took a hearty swig.

"Replanting won't take too long. Rain will soften up the ground."

Tarek harrumphed.

"How's Holland working out?" Baran asked about their newest crew member. Holland Rosenthal, or Holly as she preferred to be called, had shown up two weeks ago asking for a job to escape an arranged mating.

"She's pulling her weight," Tarek admitted with reluctance. Being old school, he didn't think it was a woman's place to be with a bunch of lumberjacks out in the middle of nowhere.

"Good. I thought she would work out." Baran bit back a smile. "The guys aren't giving her too hard of a time?"

"They are, but she gives it right back. She's feisty." A smile tugged at the corner of his mouth.

"Why don't you head up to the next site and see what we're dealing with? I don't want any surprises when we move all the equipment up there."

Tarek was an older shifter and Baran didn't want him to have a heatstroke out here in the unseasonable heat. A trip in the air-conditioned truck would cool him off.

"All right. Site forty-seven?"

"That's the one. I'm going to check that the saplings are going to be delivered on time so we can replant."

The chainsaws cut off, and a thud reverberated through the ground as another tree hit the ground.

"Probably time to move some to the burn pile."

We'd spent the last two weeks removing diseased trees that the forest management service wanted gone before more trees were infected. After the crew removed them, they were going to clear out some of the underbrush and plant the saplings.

Baran put on his hard hat and walked down the path. As he topped the ridge, he could see the machinery picking up the felled trees that had been stripped of their branches. Vonn manned the grappler and picked up the logs, placing them on the back of the semi-trailer. Everyone worked like a well-oiled machine. Jasper and Creed dragged another tree into the clearing, and Holly fired up her chainsaw to remove the limbs. With only a couple of more hours until quitting time, he needed to make sure they stayed on target. He continued down the path until he reached the truck.

Vonn killed the grappler and stepped down from the yellow machine. Sooner rather later Baran would have to replace the aging machine, but Vonn babied it to keep it working.

"One more load and trailer will be full," Vonn remarked as he walked up to Baran.

"I'll drive it down."

Baran and Vonn were almost identical, even though Vonn was the younger brother by three years. Both had dark brown hair clipped short, eyes the color of honey and golden skin. Baran was the brawnier of the two. Arms covered in tattoos were a tribute to his shifter ancestry. He kept an impressive beard, even if it made his face hotter.

Baran gazed over at his crew. He considered them a pride, even if they comprised a group of different shifters. As alpha, Baran didn't discriminate based on the shifter's animal, unlike most Alphas. Most didn't want to intermingle with other species. His group comprised mountain lions like him and his brother, bobcats, and a lynx.

"Where did Tarek run off to?" Vonn asked as he leaned against the trailer.

"Sent him up to site forty-seven to check it out."

"Good. I worry about the old goat. He's not getting any younger."

As shifters, they were long lived and didn't get sick. They could still get laid low the older they got. Baran wasn't sure how old Tarek was, but he assumed over a century judging by the gray in his hair and some of his mannerisms. It would explain why he was adamant about not hiring Holly in the beginning.

Baran himself was fifty, even though he looked to be around thirty. Holly was the youngest of the crew at the young age of twenty-seven. He managed a motley crew and had worried how they would react to a female in their midst. Not as a mate, but as an equal. To his surprise, they reacted with indifference, but time would tell if she would become one of the crew and be accepted into their group, not just a co-worker. It was unusual for a single female to join a pride without mating in.

"We're keeping a great pace here. Unless something happens, we should finish up a day early."

"You gonna let us have an extra day off?" Vonn asked hopefully.

"If it will keep you guys on track, you bet."

"Hell yeah," Vonn whooped.

"Get those logs loaded so I can get them to the burn site."

"Sure thing, boss," Vonn chuckled and dropped his hard hat back on his head.

Vonn trotted off to the grappler and fired up the diesel engine. Black smoke poured from the stack, and he picked up more logs and placed them on the trailer. Baran tossed the chains over the top of the load and secured it on the other side. After checking that everything was secured, he fired up the diesel and eased up the road they had cleared into the wooded area. By the time he returned, it was time to call it quits for the day. The sunset came earlier these days.

Vonn climbed into the passenger seat of the truck and Holly in the backseat. Creed and Jasper got into the other truck after securing the equipment in the back.

"Let's go eat," Baran said as he started up the engine.

CHAPTER 3

Lerna blinked her eyes to clear her blurry vision. Her head pounded and her mouth felt as if she had eaten a bowl of cotton. She lifted her head. Where the hell was she? The last thing she remembered was picking up her supper that her sister had sent her. After that it was a blank. The humming of tires caught her attention, and her fear spiked.

He'd found her.

A hand caressed her leg, and she shivered.

"Finally awake, Princess?" Angelo drawled from beside her.

Lerna bit her lip when he squeezed her calf hard.

"Not talking?"

"What do you want, Angelo?" Lerna croaked out.

"You, Princess. Now tell me who you've told?"

"No one. I haven't said a word."

"Don't lie to me, Princess," he bit out, his fingers digging into her flesh. Lerna couldn't hold back her whimper.

"I'm not. I haven't told anyone anything," she whispered desperate for him to believe her.

"Even your sister?"

"Especially her."

"Good girl." Angelo caressed her leg lovingly.

"Where are you taking me?"

"Some place safe. Can't have you taking off again. I don't like losing my things."

That's all she was to him. A possession. Why had she ignored the warning signs?

Because she thought she had made it.

She thought back to the first time she had seen him. Lerna had started waitressing at a popular club on the weekends. She was attending college, majoring in accounting. Her scholarship only went so far, and her parents weren't able to send her money every week. Her first night she had spilled a drink on his table, soaking his lap. Lerna expected to be fired on the spot, but he had laughed it off. He even left her a big tip. More than everyone else combined that night. Angelo returned the next night and asked her questions each time she came up to his table. She'd been flattered that a handsome man was interested in a girl as plain as her. Before he left that night, he slipped her his business card along with a hefty tip. She didn't have to eat cheap noodles the next week.

When he asked her out the following weekend, she jumped at the chance. Whenever he had free time, it was spent together. Did it bother her he would disappear for hours at a time after receiving a call? Maybe it did at first, but after a while, she figured he was a busy businessman.

Angelo showered her with gifts. New clothes and jewelry filled her small closet until it was overflowing. Her college friends were envious and made catty remarks, so when Angelo suggested she stop spending time with them, she was more than happy to do so. Her time was consumed with Angelo, school and work.

Work ended though when Angelo and his buddies got

into a fight when another guy grabbed her ass. Lerna argued she had nothing to do with it, but it fell on deaf ears. Angelo calmed her fears and convinced her to move out of her shitty apartment and live with him.

It should have set off her radar when she spent many nights alone in that apartment, but she shrugged it off. He told her that his mother enjoyed him staying at home where she could take care of her baby. The first morning he returned with a hickey on his neck should have sent her out the door. He explained it away as he had been to a business party and gotten drunk and one woman had come on to him strong. But he didn't sleep with her.

And her dumbass-self believed him.

She'd become one of those women. Her life was comfortable. All she had to focus on was school. He provided everything else for her. She didn't want to take off the rose-colored glasses.

Everything changed the night someone banged on their apartment door. Angelo was in the shower when she answered the door. She recognized the man as someone Angelo had brought over before. Marco or Matteo, Lerna couldn't remember. She didn't hesitate to let the man in.

That was a mistake.

Angelo had walked into the living room and yelled at the man in Italian. Even though Lerna did not speak the language, she could tell he was pissed. Marco grabbed her by the arm and pulled her toward him. As she struggled to get away, Enzo had come through the door with another man. They wrestled Marco to the floor.

Angelo ordered Lerna to go to their bedroom. She went but left the door open a crack to peer out. Enzo placed Marco on his knees in front of Angelo. The man pleaded in Italian, but Angelo didn't care. Another man handed Angelo a gun, and he raised it toward Marco. The sound of the shot reverberated throughout the room, and Lerna covered her mouth to smother her gasp. Enzo let go of the man and he fell to the floor. His lifeless eyes stared at Lerna as blood ran from the hole in the middle of his forehead.

She backed away from the door before the other men noticed the door wasn't closed all the way. In the bathroom, she started up the shower and stripped off her clothes. The door burst open just as she dunked her head under the water. She kept her eyes closed as the water poured down. Heat from his stare penetrated her.

Satisfied that she was unaware of what happened, he left the room. Lerna sank to the floor and sobbed. What kind of monster had she fallen for?

Lerna pretended to be asleep when he returned hours later. He climbed into bed beside her, and she squeezed her eyes shut. She didn't relax until he started snoring beside her.

The next morning, she left for class as usual, abandoning everything but her backpack, laptop and a few pieces of clothing that she could shove into her bag. Enzo drove her to campus, eyeballing her in the rearview mirror occasionally. Lerna kept her gazed fixed on the scenery outside her window. When they arrived at campus, she said her usual goodbye and walked to class. All she'd wanted to do was run as fast as she could away from him. Once inside her building, she watched from the shadows as he pulled away.

Lerna waited another fifteen minutes before she exited and strode to the quad. She emptied what she could out of the ATM, bought some bottled water and snacks. As she merged into a group of students headed to the bus stop, she dropped her phone into the trash can. She did not know where it was going, but it was taking her away from there. Lots of sleepless hours and bus transfers from local lines to national, Lerna arrived in Texas.

She thought she'd made her escape, but she now knew

differently. She was terrified she'd end up in Angelo and Enzo's clutches.

Lerna stared out the window as they merged onto the interstate. Her eyes stung with tears as she blinked them back. Tears wouldn't help anything. She needed to plan a way to get away from Angelo.

CHAPTER 4

Loud country music played in the honky-tonk as his crew laughed. It had been a long day, but the crew had busted their asses to get the job done. Baran took a pull off his beer bottle as he watched. Holly tossed a chip at Vonn for something he said. He caught the projectile and popped it into his mouth. Creed and Jasper were over at the pool table, showing some lovely ladies how to play. Even at a distance, he could smell the lust wafting from the women. Tarek sat off at a table by himself, nursing a beer and looking at his phone. Baran wondered what he was staring at since it wasn't like the old man had social media. It wouldn't be too long before he left and headed to his camper at the RV park up the road.

"Here you go, Baran," Lydia said as she placed down his plate loaded with a double cheeseburger and fries.

"Thanks."

"Need another round?"

Baran tipped up the bottle and finished the last sip.

"Please."

"Be right back." Lydia winked and turned on her heel. Her hips swayed side to side, trying to get his attention.

"She's persistent, isn't she?" Vonn commented as he pulled out a chair. He snagged a fry from Baran's plate and shoved it in his mouth.

"I think she got the hint." At least Baran hoped so.

Over the last two weeks, Lydia had made it more than obvious that she was offering more than what was on the menu. She was pretty, with her dark hair curling over her shoulders. Her red shirt clung to her curves. Normally, that would have been enough for Baran to be burning up the sheets, but he didn't get the urge.

If he hadn't been waking up rock hard every morning after dreaming of a woman he couldn't remember, he'd have been worried.

"What about you? Got one lined up for the night?" Baran asked before taking a bite of his burger.

"Not tonight," he grumbled before looking at the dance floor.

Baran followed his gaze, and it landed on Holly being twirled around by one of the locals.

"Ah hell, Vonn," Baran remarked.

"Don't worry. Nothing will come of it." He drummed his fingers on the table, eyes fixed on Holly.

"Does she know?"

"No," Vonn bit out.

Vonn was a rare breed amongst shifters. An outcast among a lot of prides. He could hide parts of his scent or all of it if he wished. He was also more in touch with the world and sometimes he 'knew' things. It made other shifters skittish if they found out. In this case, he was concealing the scent that would tell Holly he was her fated mate.

"She's had enough shit to deal with. I'm not going to burden her."

"Burden?" Baran blurted out. "Shifters pray that they'll find their fated one. Most never do." Gods knew Baran hadn't.

"Not her," Vonn grumbled. "I overheard her, and she doesn't want anything to do with mating."

"Her asshole father is to blame for that. If he hadn't tried to force her to mate who he wanted, it would be different."

"If I ever get my hands on him," Vonn threatened, balling his hand into a fist.

"If he hadn't, you may never have met her," Baran advised.

"Damn, I don't want any reason to be beholden to that man."

"She'll come around. Eventually."

"How long will I have to wait? I'm nearly fifty," Vonn complained.

"Good thing you have another hundred years or so," Baran replied bitterly. Baran had been looking for his fated one for as long as he could remember. In his younger years, he was an average shifter with a high sex drive, but the excess of women became old. He wanted his one.

"Baran, I'm sorry," Vonn apologized. He knew of his brother's wish. "I wasn't thinking. This isn't your problem. You're right. Give it a few years and she'll come around. I just hope she's still here when she does."

Baran nursed the beer that Lydia had dropped off. Jealousy had risen inside Baran that his baby brother had found his fated one. He'd been looking for years, and Vonn's fell into his lap. Fate was a fickle bitch.

Baran felt a tug in his chest and absently rubbed his hand across it.

"Don't let her get away, Vonn. You've only got this one shot. You need to change her mind."

Vonn looked away and twirled his empty beer bottle.

"But go easy on her. It can't be easy to abandon everything she knew defying her father."

"It's going to happen for you too, Baran. You need to have faith."

"I'm getting a little old to be counting on faith, brother. I'm outta here. See you back at camp."

Baran stood from the table.

Vonn clamped his hand around his forearm in a bruising grip, a far-off look in his eyes.

"Never. She's out there waiting for you."

CHAPTER 5

Night had fallen. Bustling city had turned into small rural towns and now they were in the middle of nowhere. She'd lost count of the hours she's been stuck in the back seat with Angelo. They hadn't passed another car for at least ten minutes. The headlights illuminated the road in front of them. Out the side window, Lerna stared into the darkness.

"I need to use the bathroom," Lerna murmured.

"Hold it," Angelo barked out.

"I can't hold it anymore. It's been hours. If you don't want me to pee all over this seat, you better pull over!"

Angelo bit out a curse in Italian.

"Enzo, find a spot to pull over."

Dark eyes met Lerna's in the rearview mirror and flashed with what looked like guilt. Enzo eased over to the side of the road. Tires crunched on the loose gravel as they came to a stop. Angelo threw open his door with a curse. He disappeared into the night until he came around and pulled open her door. He grabbed her arm in a bruising grip and yanked her from the vehicle. Lerna's bare feet slipped on the loose gravel. She scrabbled for purchase but lost to gravity. Her knees slammed into the unforgiving asphalt.

"Get up," Angelo ground out, pulling her arm.

Lerna bit back a retort. She couldn't make him any madder. Who knew what he would do to her? She got her feet under her and slowly stood. She peered into the darkened woods in front of her. A spike of fear gripped her. What beasts lurked in the darkness? Was she any safer with the beast at her side? She'd take her chances in the dark.

"Got any napkins?"

"For what?"

"Unlike you, I can't just whip something out and shake it off. I don't want to drip dry."

Angelo cursed and snapped his fingers at Enzo. The man miraculously produced a wad of white paper and placed it in her hand. Lerna stepped toward the woods, Angelo dogging her steps.

"A little privacy, please?"

"No," Angelo barked out.

"Really? You want to watch me pee?"

"I'm keeping my eyes on you."

"Where do you think I'm going to go?" Lerna retorted. "We're in the middle of nowhere. We haven't passed a car or house in forever!"

"Fine. Don't go far. You won't like it if I have to come after you," Angelo warned, squeezing her arm.

Lerna flinched and Angelo smiled, an evil glint in his dark eyes. She headed into the darkness, making as much noise as she could because silence would be imperative if she was going to escape. The tall grass brushed her legs as she stopped. When she reached the tree line, she weaved between two closely placed trunks.

"That's far enough," Angelo yelled out.

"Okay, just give me a minute."

Lerner made some rustling sounds as if she were dropping her pants and after a few seconds hurried into the darkness. She bit back her fear of the unknown. She focused all getting away from the man behind her, one who was probably going to kill her for what she had seen.

Tree branches slapped at her skin, snagged in her long hair, but she pressed on. She hesitated when something howled in the distance, way too close for her liking.

"Get it together," she whispered to herself. "It's more afraid of you than you are of it."

Lerna kept her arms outstretched in front of her to avoid running smack dab into a tree as the inky blackness encompassed her vision. She glanced behind her and not even the headlights from the SUV were visible.

"Lerna!" Angelo bellowed.

Even at a distance, it caused a frisson of fear to race down her spine. Despite the darkness, she took off running, praying she was far enough away that he wouldn't hear her footsteps on the soft forest floor. After an eternity, the ground started to slope upwards, and she scrabbled for purchase. The trees cleared as she stepped onto the asphalt. Right into the path of headlights.

CHAPTER 6

Baran climbed into his truck and fired it up. Vonn could catch a ride with one of the other guys back to the RV park. He needed a few moments alone to feel sorry for himself. Later, he would thank the Gods above that his baby brother had found his fated one, even if she didn't know it.

Gravel crunched under his tires as he pulled out of his spot and swung onto the road. Garth Brooks sang about *Friends in Low Places* as he drummed his fingers on the steering wheel. He turned on the road that led to the park, headlights shining into the darkness. As he rounded a bend in the road, his phone slid from the seat onto the floor. Reaching down, he picked it up, eyes leaving the road for just a second. When he looked back up, a woman stood in the middle of the road. He stomped on the brakes and yanked the steering wheel to the left.

Baran's breath came in harsh pants as he rocked to a stop. He threw the truck into park and threw open the door. He prayed to the Gods that whoever she was and, for whatever fucking reason, she was standing in the middle of the road, that she was all right.

He rounded the back end of the truck and slid to a stop. She stood there, dark hair blowing in the breeze and green eyes wide. Blood dripped down her cheek, but she didn't seem to notice.

"Hey, are you okay?"

His voice seemed to break her out of whatever trance she was in. Eyes closing, her knees buckled. Baran shot forward and caught her before she landed on the asphalt. As his arms wrapped around her, he inhaled her scent. Overriding the scent of her terror was the undeniable scent of his mate. His fated one.

"Damn, Vonn. You were right, little brother," Baran breathed out.

The one thing Baran didn't scent was her animal. Fate was laughing at him. He'd hoped and prayed for years to find his fated one, but little did he know that she'd be human.

Humans, as a rule, generally knew nothing of shifters. It had kept them safe for as long as they'd walked the earth. Humans feared what they didn't understand, and shifters didn't want to become lab rats for the human governments to experiment on. It was rare that a human was the fated mate of a shifter.

Vonn was going to laugh his ass off when he found out.

She felt slight in his arms as he lifted her. Scratches and welts peppered her face and arms, and her pants were ripped at her knees. Smelling her blood infuriated his cat. He gathered her close to his chest and walked to the passenger side of his truck. He placed her down on the seat.

"Can you hear me?" he asked softly so as not to startle her.

Her brow furrowed before she blinked her eyes open. Eyes the color of fresh pine needles met his and widened. She scrambled across the seat away from him.

"Easy. You're alright. I'm not going to hurt you," Baran

soothed her. He looked down and saw the blood streaking his leather seats.

"Are you hurt?"

"I, ugh, I don't know," she breathed out. "I think-"

From behind him, he heard someone shout, and he turned to look. She whimpered.

"Not friends of yours, I take it?"

She shook her head.

"Buckle up and I'll get us out of here."

Baran slammed the door shut and ran around the front of the cab. When he climbed in, he noticed she'd buckled her belt but had crouched down in the seat. As he put the truck into drive, he glanced over her head and saw two men burst out of the trees, guns drawn. He stomped on the gas, causing the truck to fishtail. Bullets peppered the side of his truck and tailgate as he pulled away. She whimpered from beside him and covered her head with her hands.

"Hold on!"

Baran turned off the truck's lights, plunging them into darkness. The canopy of trees overhead helped his black truck blend into the night. With his enhanced night vision, Baran easily navigated the turns in the road. The men continued to fire, but could not hit their target with accuracy as he wove across the lanes. The woman continued to tremble in the seat beside him. Little mewling sounds escaped her tightly pressed lips. Baran reached over and grabbed her hand, and squeezed. She clasped his hand tight and held on like it was her lifeline.

"It's okay. You're safe now. I won't let them hurt you," Baran promised. "My name's Baran."

"Lerna," she got out between her chattering teeth.

He realized that her adrenaline was wearing off and shock was setting in. Dropping her hand, he reached into the back seat and grabbed a flannel shirt that had been riding around back there. He draped it over her. It swamped her frame. She curled her fingers around the edge and pulled it tighter around herself.

"Well, Lerna, it's nice to meet you, but I wish it was under better circumstances."

She barked out a laugh.

"We're about half an hour from the sheriff's office-"

"No cops."

"Hun, those men just chased you through the woods and shot at us," he reminded her.

"No cops," Lerna reiterated. "He has cops in his pockets."

"Not down here," he remarked, noting her accent. Definitely not local. "Where did you come from?"

She bit her lip and looked away.

"Lerna, help me out here."

"Please, no cops."

"Fine," Baran uttered. "Where do you want me to take you? A motel?"

She shook her head and reached over for his hand. Her touch soothed him and his cat, who was pacing inside him.

"I can take you back with me."

Big green eyes looked at him, full of hope.

"You'll be safe with me."

She nodded her head and leaned back against the seat with his shirt tucked around her. His cat purred in contentment.

The sound of the tires on the road lulled her to sleep, and she slumped against his shoulder. The air conditioner ruffled her hair, stirring her scent in the cab. Baran dropped his hand and rubbed it up and down her arm to satisfy his need to comfort his mate. She sighed and leaned heavier into him.

Too soon for his liking, the lights of the RV park came into view. He tuned on the gravel driveway and passed several parked vehicles before reaching the back of the lot where his was parked. The lights weren't on, and he assumed Vonn hadn't made it here before him. Baran killed the engine, the ticking sound of the engine loud inside of the truck.

He waited for her to stir, but she continued to sleep. Everything had caught up with her, he guessed. He opened his door and eased out. Lerna leaned into the seat with a quiet moan. He rounded the front of the truck and opened the passenger side door.

"Lerna," he said, patting her leg.

Her face pulled into a frown, and she swatted at him.

"Sleepy," she muttered.

Baran chuckled. He left the door open and went to his home away from home. He unlocked the door and swung it open until it caught the outside latch. Hoping Vonn had picked up after himself for once, he flipped the switch, turning on the light, then walked back to the truck. He unbuckled her seat belt and eased his arms underneath her.

"Lerna, put your arms around my neck."

Green eyes peeked out beneath long dark lashes as she complied. Her head came to rest on his shoulder. Baran was thankful that he built a wider and sturdier set of steps up into his trailer as he carried her inside. He walked toward the front where his bed was. He shouldered the door open and placed her on top of the covers. She made a little shuffling noise and buried her head in his pillow. He grabbed a blanket from the end of the bed and placed it on her. Easing back, he looked at her in his bed.

Finally, everything seemed right in Baran's world. His cat preened at the sight of their mate in their den. He left the door open a crack and sat down at the table.

How the hell was he going to explain this to his crew?

CHAPTER 7

Baran was on his second beer when the sound of a truck approaching caught his attention. Vonn spoke with someone and slammed the door shut. His footsteps seemed abnormally loud as he walked up the steps and Baran craned his head to see if he woke Lerna.

Vonn opened the door and froze with a look of shock on his face.

"You dog," he chuckled. "You need me to bunk with the guys?"

"No, you're fine."

"Why are you out here and not in there?" He inclined his head toward the door. "Refueling for round two?" His face creased into a sloppy, drunk grin.

"Shut it, Vonn."

"Shouldn't you be in a better mood if you got laid?" Vonn leaned back against the counter. It was tight quarters with the two of them in the kitchenette.

"I said shut it," Baran growled out.

Vonn bowed his head.

"Sorry, Alpha," he uttered.

Baran ran a hand across the back of his neck.

"It's fine."

"What's the deal, bro? I'm just giving you shit, you know that. I'm surprised really. You rarely bring anyone home."

"She's mine, Vonn."

"Yours?" his brow furrowed but popping up in surprise. "Really? No shit?" With that realization, Vonn sobered up fast.

"No shit." He took another drink of his beer.

Vonn sniffed the air.

"Human? Damn, bro. Why do I smell blood?"

"I almost ran her over on the way home. She was standing in the middle of the road."

"You hit her?!" Vonn yelped.

"I said almost. I swerved in time. She was running from two guys. I guess you're too drunk to notice the bullet holes in my truck?"

"They fucking shot at you!?" His golden eyes widened.

"Yes. I got us the hell out of there. She fell asleep in the truck and hasn't woken up yet."

"Is she shot? Do we need to take her to a human place?" Vonn paced back and forth in the small space.

"Human place? You mean a hospital?"

"Yeah that. Come on, we need to get her in the truck!" Vonn yelled and turned. He stumbled and fell against the table.

"You need to sober up. Drink some water," Baran ordered. "She wasn't shot. She ran through the woods barefoot and got some cuts and scratches."

"Why didn't you clean her up?"

"One, she was scared. Two, she passed out in the truck. I don't think she'd want a stranger putting his hands all over her. Three, I think she needs the rest more than getting clean. And keep it down. I don't want her to wake up to you yelling like a damn drunken fool," Baran ground out.

"Sorry," Vonn whispered.

"Go to bed, Vonn," he breathed out. "We'll talk in the morning."

"You want to bunk with me?"

"No, I'm going to hang out here. I don't want her to freak out in the middle of the night."

"You don't think waking up in a strange bed is going to freak her out?"

"It might, but at least I'll be out here to know. Now go."

Vonn shuffled to the back of the trailer and opened the door to his room. Baran had taken out the original bunk beds that were on each side of the room and put in a queen size platform bed with storage for his brother to use. Vonn must have drunk his weight in alcohol to be that intoxicated. It took a lot to have an effect on shifters. Baran wondered what made his brother drink to excess. He was sure Holly was involved.

Baran heard the whisper of cloth move from his room. Eyes fixated on the open door, he waited to see if she'd wake or settle back into a deep sleep. He was equally hopeful and terrified. He'd heard the change in her breathing and heart rate when he and Vonn were talking. He wasn't sure how much she had heard of their conversation, but he would have a lot of explaining to do when they came face to face again.

CHAPTER 8

Lerna clutched the blanket to her chin and stared into the darkness of the room. A sliver of light revealed the opened doorway. She had woken when the other man had come in.

But come in where?

Where the hell was she?

The last thing she remembered was the man putting her in his truck and driving off.

Oh God. Angelo and Enzo had shot at them! She jerked up; the blanket clutched to her chest. Her eyes darted around the darkened room as if Angelo was going to appear out of thin air.

"Get a freaking grip," she whispered to herself.

The other man crashed into something, and Baran ordered him to go to bed. Surprisingly, the man did as he was told.

Lerna laid back down and shifted until she found a comfortable position. A spicy scent drifted up from the pillow as she placed her cheek on it. It lulled her into a sense of peace, and she drifted back off to sleep.

The next time she opened her eyes, dull light was leaking out from the curtains. She stretched her arms and hit the shelf at the head of the bed. Something rattled at the contact and she froze. The events of yesterday crashed over her. Angelo finding her and taking her to God knows where to do God knows what. Her mad dash through the woods and almost ending up as roadkill, only to be saved by her knight in shining armor. Or blue jeans. It didn't matter. All she knew was that for the moment she was safe. Now she had to worry about staying that way.

The sound of dishes clanking together reminded her of the fact she wasn't alone, and she had dragged another innocent person into danger.

He had to be angry at her. Bullet holes riddled his poor truck. Each time one had hit the vehicle, she had waited for the pain. Baran had gotten them out of there by the skin of their teeth. She bit down on her thumb. What the hell was she supposed to do now?

A knock on the door drew her out of her pity party.

"Yes?" she croaked out.

The door opened slowly. Baran filled the doorway. She sucked in a breath. Last night she hadn't gotten a good look at him, but hot damn. He had his dark hair cut short, which accentuated his amber eyes. A full thick beard covered the lower part of his face but framed his full lips. He wore a light gray t-shirt with the letters RTM sandwiched between a tree and chainsaw on the upper right chest area, covering his broad chest. He crossed his arms, and the sleeves stretched until she thought the seams would unravel from the strain. Dark images covered his arms, and she could make out some sort of wild animal. Her eyes ventured lower until she came to the noticeable bulge covered by weathered denim.

Baran cleared his throat, and her face flamed.

What the hell was she doing?

"Sleep well?" he asked teasingly.

"Yes, surprisingly." She kneaded the blanket, refusing to meet his eyes. "You?"

"I slept okay. I've been working on breakfast if you want to get cleaned up."

She reached up to run her fingers through her hair and found a mass of snarls. She touched something hard and pulled out a small twig from a tree.

She must have looked like a hot mess.

"The hot water tank isn't very big, but it'll get the job done. I don't have any girly soap or anything for you to use," he admitted.

"I'm grateful for anything. I must look horrible."

"You're beautiful."

"Yeah right," she snorted out a laugh, but her gaze caught his. Nothing but honesty shone in those eyes. He thought she was beautiful. "Ugh, thank you."

"You can wear a pair of my shorts and a shirt. They'll be too big, but they'll work until we can get you something else." He moved over to a small set of drawers and pulled out the items. He turned and handed them to her. Their hands touched, and she flinched from the contact but didn't let go. Warmth flowed from where her skin touched his. His eyes seemed to flash golden for a brief second, but returning to their beautiful amber color.

"Thank you."

"You're welcome," he replied, his voice husky. Did he feel it too?

"For all of it. You didn't have to stop last night."

"What kind of male would I be if I had left you standing on the side of the road? My mother would have had my ass beaten."

"You risked your life for me. You could have been killed. It's bad enough that your truck was shot up. Somehow, I'll pay you back," Lerna promised.

"Hush. Don't worry about any of that now. You'll feel better once you get cleaned up. There're some bandages and ointment in the grocery bag on the sink if you need it."

"What? Why?"

"You got a little banged up on your trek through the woods."

He smiled, and her breath caught. It should be illegal to look that good.

"Breakfast should be done in about ten minutes." He backed out of the room as if he was afraid to take his eyes off her.

Was he afraid she would steal something?

She snorted. Not like she could hide anything with what she was wearing.

She moved to the edge of the bed, and her body ached. Her feet touched the floor, and she hissed as she put her weight on them. Baran appeared in the doorway, startlingly her into falling back on the bed.

"What's wrong?"

"My feet."

He stooped and lifted her leg. His thumb caressed her ankle as he looked her foot over. His brows furrowed.

"They're pretty scratched up and I think you may have some stickers in there. I should have checked last night. I'm sorry."

"Stickers?"

"Little thorns. Come on, I'll carry you, then I'll see if I can get them out. I can't see anything with all the dirt."

Her face flamed with embarrassment at being dirty. He scooped her up before she could utter a protest.

"Arms around my neck, angel."

She placed her arms on his shoulders and rested her cheek on his chest like it was second nature. He maneuvered them through the doorway toward the narrow hallway. He stopped at a closed door.

"Can you get the handle?" He nodded to the door.

She reached over, and it swung open when she turned the knob. The bathroom was small, but surprisingly clean and not smelly. She'd had to clean the men's bathroom at the club before and knew how bad it could smell. How men could miss the toilet when they could aim always surprised her.

He placed her on the closed toilet seat and reached into the shower and turned it on.

"It'll take a minute for the water to get hot. There's body wash on the shelf."

He brushed her legs as he turned and opened the cabinet door. He pulled out a white towel and washcloth.

"Do you need me to help you?"

"I think I can manage, but thank you."

"Damn, I forgot your clothes. I'll be right back."

Steam formed in the shower enclosure, and she stood, trying to keep her weight on the outside of her feet. She winced, but the pain was manageable. She glanced in the mirror and gasped in horror. Her hair was a rat's nest with leaves and other things sticking out. A nasty gash bisected her cheek and blood had dried where it had dripped down. Welts and other scratches peppered her arms. The same with her stomach, where her skin was unprotected. Her pants were ripped at the knees from where she had fallen, and the pink fabric was stuck into the abrasions on her knees.

"Holy shit. What the hell was he thinking when he said I was beautiful?" she muttered to herself.

CHAPTER 9

"Because you are." His voice sounded from behind her.

He'd moved so quietly that she jumped with a squeal.

"Sorry, I didn't mean to scare you."

"It's fine. I'm a little jumpy still. For a big guy, you don't make a lot of noise."

"I'm light on my feet." He smiled, and she wanted to melt into a puddle of goo at his feet. "Here are the clothes. There's an extra toothbrush and a comb in the cabinet."

"Thanks." He backed out and pulled the door shut.

Lerna stripped off her clothes and got into the small enclosure. The hot water felt heavenly as it pelted her sore muscles. Picking up the three in one soap men seemed to favor, she dropped a large dollop on the rag and squished it to make a lather. She rubbed her face and hissed as the soap stung the open scrapes and scratches.

"You okay?" The door muffled Baran's voice.

"I'm fine," she called back. "How the heck did you even hear that? Are you standing outside the door?"

"I've got good hearing. And yes, I'm standing out here in case you need something."

"That's not creepy at all," she muttered. His booming laugh made her smile.

"Not trying to be creepy. I wasn't sure how strong you were this morning. I didn't want you to fall in there and hurt yourself."

"I appreciate your concern, but I'm fine."

"If you say so. I'll finish up breakfast. Anything you don't like?"

"Not really."

The wall groaned as he pushed off. Lerna breathed out a sigh of relief. What if she had done something embarrassing like farting? She never would have been able to look him in the eye. And he had pretty eyes. Hazel flecked with amber framed with long dark lashes.

Did she really think they had glowed last night in the dark?

She shook her head at the silly thought. She'd been out of her head with fright. Seeing things that weren't there.

When she turned off the water and grabbed the towel, she detected the heavenly aroma of bacon frying. Her stomach growled in response. She toweled off and threw on the clothes that he left for her. The shirt fell to her knees. The shorts were loose in the waist, but for once she was happy for her wide hips as they kept them from falling off. She found the comb and toothbrush. She brushed her teeth with the minty paste until her mouth no longer felt like it was coated in a layer of grime. The comb, however, was pointless. Her hair was gnarled and without conditioner there wasn't a chance in hell that she was getting the tangles out. With a huff of frustration, she put the comb back into the cabinet. She pulled open the door and ran into a hard chest.

"Easy there," a voice chuckled.

The voice was like Baran's, but not. She looked up into an

almost identical version of Baran. Instead of a beard, he sported a neatly trimmed goatee, and he had pulled back his hair into a ponytail.

"Sorry."

"No worries, darlin'. Space is a little tight around here. I'm Vonn, Baran's brother."

"Lerna."

"Pleasure to meet you, Lerna. Why don't you turn left and head for the kitchen and let me in the bathroom?"

"Oh yes, sorry." Lerna felt her face heat.

She squeezed past Vonn and made her way to the small kitchen. Baran was standing over the stove, flipping bacon in a pan. Her mouth watered as the delicious smell filled her nose. He turned and gave her a smile.

"Coffee?" he asked, pointing to the table where a freshly brewed pot of coffee sat.

"Yes, please," she said, sliding onto the bench seat.

She poured herself a cup of coffee and took a sip, feeling the hot liquid warm her up inside.

"Thanks," she said, looking up at him.

"No problem," he said, returning her gaze before giving her a once over. "You look good in my clothes."

Lerna blushed at the compliment, feeling a warmth spread through her body that had nothing to do with the coffee. What was the deal with these men? She'd never been as flustered in her life.

"Thank you," she said, her voice barely above a whisper. "Sorry if I look a mess." She raised a hand to her tangled hair.

"Don't worry about it," Baran said, turning back to the stove. "I've got plenty of extra clothes if you need them. Plus, it's not every day I get to share my clothes with a beautiful woman."

Lerna nearly choked on her coffee at his words. She couldn't believe he was saying these things to her. She'd seen herself in the mirror. A hot mess was what she was.

Baran's gaze intensified, and Lerna wondered if he could read her thoughts. She shifted uncomfortably on the bench, suddenly feeling exposed in a way that had nothing to do with her appearance.

Just then, Vonn walked into the kitchen, his hair still wet from the shower. He gave Lerna a friendly nod before heading over to the stove and helping himself to a piece of bacon.

"Get out of the food, you ass," Baron rebuked his brother.

Vonn turned and winked at her. Lerna breathed a sigh of relief, grateful for the distraction. As she sipped her coffee, she couldn't help but notice the similarities between the two men. Both were easy on the eyes, but Baran was in a more rugged way. She watched the play of muscles in his back and arms as he cooked. She'd never thought of a back as sexy before, but he was changing her mind. To ward off the sudden heat pooling in her core, she shifted her legs.

Baron seemed to raise his head and deeply inhale before looking at her over his shoulder. His eyes flashed gold for a brief second.

"And I'm out of here," Vonn remarked grabbing another piece of bacon and shoving it in his mouth.

Baran's eyes never left hers as Vonn left.

She fidgeted.

"That sure smells good," she offered, looking down at her cup.

"Damn right it does," he replied, his voice deeper than before.

Her gaze flashed back to him, and she knew he wasn't talking about the bacon. Her heart fluttered in her chest.

Baran took the bacon off the stove and turned to face her, his eyes still holding hers captive. Lerna felt a shiver run down her spine as he strode toward her, his presence filling up the tiny space. He stopped right in front of her, so close that she could smell the soap on his skin. The air between them crackled with tension, and Lerna felt her pulse racing in her veins.

"Baran..." she whispered, her voice barely audible.

He said nothing, just reached out and took her coffee cup from her hand, placing it on the table in front of her. Then he cupped her face in his large hands, letting his thumb brush over her lips. Lerna felt her breath hitch in her throat, her eyes locked onto his.

"Last night was pretty intense," he said finally, his voice gravelly.

Lerna nodded, unable to speak. Her heart was pounding so hard she thought it might burst out of her chest.

"Do you want to talk about what happened?"

Reality crashed back into Lerna, and she eased back from his touch.

"The less you know, the better."

CHAPTER 10

As soon as she pulled back from his touch, Baran felt cold.

"Lerna, you're safe with me."

She shook her head, eyes full of defeat, and looked at the table. Her finger traced a pattern on the laminate.

"You don't understand," she croaked out. She cleared her throat. "So, what's the plan for today?" she asked.

Baran turned back to the stove and cracked a couple of eggs into the skillet. The bacon grease crackled and popped.

"Well, unless you have any objections, I thought we could head into town and restock on some supplies. Maybe find you some better clothes," he replied.

"That sounds good," she said, trying to sound enthusiastic, but it fell flat to his ears.

An uncomfortable silence fell between them as he finished cooking. He plated up the breakfast. Lerna watched as he arranged the bacon and eggs on two plates before setting them on the table. They ate in comfortable silence, the only sounds being the clinking of their silverware on the plates.

Lerna pushed her plate away with a groan and Baran

smiled in satisfaction, knowing he was taking care of his mate. He stood and cleared their dirty dishes from the table.

"Thank you. It was delicious."

"Want to hit the road? It'll take about forty-five minutes until the nearest town with a decent sized store."

"I guess."

They went outside to see Vonn sitting in a lawn chair with his feet kicked up on a wooden table.

"Taking your truck, Vonn."

"I noticed you acquired some new holes in the ass end of yours." Vonn tossed him the keys.

"Just another night on the town." He laughed.

Lerna grabbed his arm. "Are you sure it's safe for me to go out?"

"If I wasn't, I'd keep your cute rear end here and send Vonn to get you stuff."

She bit down on her lower lip, and he ached to trace it with his tongue.

Baran shook his head, chasing away those thoughts. He needed to focus on keeping her safe, not on his desire for her. He opened the door for her and helped her into the passenger seat of the truck before walking around to the driver's side.

As they drove toward town, Baran couldn't help but steal glances at Lerna out of the corner of his eye. She looked lost in thought, her eyes staring out at the passing scenery as she chewed on her thumbnail. He wanted to grill her about last night, but he didn't want to push her if she wasn't ready to talk.

They arrived in town, and Baran parked the truck in front of the store. He turned to Lerna. "Ready to go shopping?"

She gave him a small smile and nodded, so they got out of the truck and headed inside. As they walked down the aisles, Lerna kept close to him, her hand gripping his arm. Baran could feel her trembling slightly.

"What do you want to get first?"

"Conditioner," she answered, fingering her hair that she had in a messy bun on top of her head.

Baron directed her toward the beauty aisle. While she perused the many bottles lining the shelves, he stood by the cart. He did not know what half the bottles meant. He usually grabbed a bottle of stuff and went on his way. She picked up a bottle of the cheapest stuff and placed it in the cart.

"Is that any good?"

She wrinkled her nose before answering. "It's fine."

He picked up the bottle and looked at the label. Going to the shelf, he looked over the selections and found the same one with a higher price. He placed the cheap bottle on the shelf and picked up the more expensive one, along with the shampoo beside it.

"This work?" He showed her the bottle.

"Yes, but-"

He stopped her short. "What's next? Soap? Lotion?"

"Baran, the cheaper stuff will work. You don't need to get that one."

He hushed her with a look.

"Soap," she muttered.

A few minutes later, he loaded the cart with body wash, a poofy sponge thing, and a bottle of lotion. He steered the cart to the women's section. Lerna blushed when he stopped in the underwear section.

"Need any help to pick things out?" he teased.

The look she gave him would have slayed a lesser man.

"I think I can handle it."

Baran stayed on the outer aisle while she disappeared. She returned with a package of bikini underwear, socks, and two bras. Even though she chose plain cotton with no frills, he couldn't help but picture her wearing them. He shook his head to clear his thoughts.

She dropped them into the cart.

He led her deeper into the women's sections. She rifled

through the selection of shirt and pants. She picked out a couple of plain t-shirts and jeans. He added a zip up hoodie to the pile.

"Anything else?" he asked.

"Maybe some shoes?"

He glanced down at her feet, which looked tiny in his borrowed flip flops.

"I think that's a great idea."

After selecting a pair of plain sneakers, she dropped them on top of the clothing.

"That everything?"

Lerna nodded. "I think so."

"Okay, let's head to the checkout, then."

As they approached the register, Lerna tensed up and started fidgeting with her fingers. Her eyes darted around the other customers. Baran noticed her discomfort and placed his hand on the small of her back, rubbing soothing circles. She leaned into his touch, and he felt ten feet tall.

As the cashier scanned their items, Baran couldn't help but notice the way the man's eyes lingered on Lerna's body. He felt a surge of possessiveness, his cat snarling within him. When they finished checking out, Baran took the bags from the cashier and steered Lerna toward the exit.

"Let's go," he said, eager to get her out of there.

As they exited, Baran scanned the parking lot for any threat. His cat was on high alert. He ushered her into the truck and started the engine. They pulled out on to Main Street that went through the center of town. Lerna stared out the window, watching the people milling about on the sidewalk. She gasped and grabbed his arm. Baran turned to look as she ducked lower in the seat.

CHAPTER 11

Her breath caught in her chest as she saw Angelo and Enzo walking down the sidewalk, side by side with the innocent people of this small town.

"What is it?" Baran asked, eyes darting across the road.

Angelo and Enzo had tried to blend in with the townsfolk and had ditched their button up shirts and thousand-dollar leather loafers. She almost didn't recognize them in jeans and polos. However, they couldn't disguise the air of arrogance and evil that permeated their pores. Lerna felt the sweat bead at her temples as she watched them. Her heart was pounding so hard she feared it would burst out of her chest. She knew that if they saw her, she would lead them right to Baran and Vonn.

"It's them," she whispered.

"From last night?" She felt the truck slow.

"No, don't stop. Keep going. They can't see us," she hissed.

Baran looked like he wanted to jump out and confront them, but nodded and eased his foot down on the pedal, pulling away from Angelo and Enzo. Lerna watched them disappear through the back window. She breathed a sigh of relief and leaned back into her seat, closing her eyes to calm down. She trembled with fear, knowing that they were that close. What had she thought? That she had escaped, and they just gave up? She'd seen them kill a man. She didn't breathe normally until she saw them pass the city limits sign.

"I think you need to tell me what's going on, Lerna. What kind of trouble are you in?"

Baran's profile caught her attention once again, and she couldn't help but feel strongly attracted to him. No, attraction was too tame a word for what she felt. She had never felt drawn to someone like she felt towards Baran. He made her want to bare her soul.

"If I told you, you'd be in as much trouble as I am."

"Were those cops, Feds?"

"The opposite actually." She laughed at the thought of them being law enforcement.

"If I don't know what's going on, I can't keep you safe," he ground out.

"It's not your job, Baran. It's better for both of us if I get as far away from here that I can before they find me again."

He slammed on the brakes. The scent of burnt rubber filled the truck cab. He yanked the wheel until the truck was half on the road and half in the grass.

"You listen to me," he ordered, taking her chin in his hand.

"It's more than my job," he growled.

Honest to God, it sounded like he growled. His eyes flashed a bright gold. She didn't imagine it this time.

"What do you mean?" she whispered.

"You tell me your secrets and I'll tell you mine. Mine will be a hell of a lot harder to believe."

Her hand circled his wrist, thumb grazing the underside. His pulse was pounding a mile a minute.

"Mind if we make a little detour?" He looked anxious.

"Sure."

He eased back onto the road and took a left at the next intersection. They drove until there were nothing but soaring trees lining the road, their leaves creating a canopy over the narrow road. Another turn sent them down a gravel road that ended at a wide-open area where trees had been level down to short stumps.

"What happened here?" Lerna asked, as Baran pulled to a stop at the top of a small hill.

"This is our work site."

"You cut down all these trees?" At his nod, she asked, "Why?"

"Disease. We were hired to come in and cut down all the trees that were infected. It's a disease that spreads and kills the trees. They needed to be removed."

"It's so empty."

"We'll replant saplings before we leave, so the area will look like it did before in a decade."

"You're a lumberjack?"

"Yes. We work in timber management. My crew and I travel around the country clearing land."

"You're the head guy?"

"In more ways than one," he muttered. "Yes, I own the company. Vonn and a few others work for me."

"Where's home?"

"It's a small town a couple of hours from here. We take the RVs and stay in the area where we're working."

"How long does this take?" Lerna pointed at the stumps protruding from the ground.

"It depends on the size of the job. This one is a couple of months. We come in, cut down the trees and haul them off to be destroyed. Once the area is cleared, we'll plant the saplings and move on to the next contract."

Baran killed the engine and opened his door. Lerna unbuckled her belt and stepped out of the truck. The surrounding silence was comforting. The occasional sound of leaves rustling in the breeze and birds chirping had her relaxing slightly for the first time since that night. He pulled the handle on the tailgate, and it drop with a thud. He turned to face Lerna and placed his hands on her hips. Her skin felt electrified at his touch. Lerna looked up into his eyes and didn't need to wonder if he felt it, too. It was plain to see on his face. He lifted her up and sat her down on the warmed metal. Baran settled between her parted thighs.

Lerna felt her heart racing as Baran leaned in to place a soft kiss on her lips. It was a gentle kiss, almost hesitant, but it sent shivers down her spine. She felt his hand brush against her cheek as he deepened the kiss, his tongue probing into her mouth. It was like a dam had broken inside her, and she felt the pent-up desire and longing rushing to the surface.

Baran's hands roamed over her body, tracing the curves of her hips and waist, and she moaned into his mouth. She could feel the heat emanating from his body, and it made her feel alive in a way she had never experienced before.

For a moment, she forgot about the danger that was lurking around them and lost herself in the moment.

As their lips parted, Baran looked at her with a hunger that made her core ache. "I know we just met, but I can't resist you," he whispered hoarsely.

"I don't understand. Why do I feel this way about you?"

"It's one of the secrets I'll tell you."

Lerna looked out over the valley below.

"Let me tell you a story about a naive girl who thought she met her dream guy. He was attentive and giving. She ignored the red flags. He made her dependent on him and pulled her away from her friends until he was the only thing she had."

"Where did she meet him?" The truck dipped when he sat down beside her. He took her hand in his and twined their fingers together. His touch gave her the strength to carry on.

"In a club where she worked to pay her bills while she was in college."

"A smart girl."

"A dumb, smart girl. She didn't realize until too late what he really was. The monster that he is."

"What made her see?"

"She saw him kill a man."

Baran's grip on Lerna's hand tightened. "You saw him kill someone?"

"Yes," Lerna whispered, tears welling up in her eyes. "I didn't know what to do, so I ran. Now they're after me. They won't stop until they find me."

Baran's grip on her hand tightened. Lerna closed her eyes, trying to push the memories to the back of her mind.

"I was scared, terrified. I didn't know what to do, so I ran. I left everything behind and thought I'd be safe if I just kept moving."

"But they found you."

Lerna nodded, her eyes still closed. "Somehow, they always find me. I don't know how they do it."

Baran pulled her closer, wrapping his arms around her in a protective embrace.

"You don't have to be scared anymore. I'll keep you safe."

Lerna's eyes snapped open, and she pulled back slightly to look at him. "You don't even know me. Why do you care?"

Baran's eyes met hers, his expression unwavering. "I care because you're mine."

CHAPTER 12

"Yours?" Lerna breathed out. "I don't understand."

Baran rose from the truck and paced in front of her. He jerked his head toward the valley and started walking, hoping she'd follow. Baran walked a few steps ahead of her, further into the clearing. He turned around and looked at her.

"I don't want to scare you, but I think it's time I tell you the truth about who I am."

"Besides a lumberjack?" She chuckled.

Baran fumbled with what to say. He'd never told a human he was a mountain lion shifter. He took a deep breath and spoke.

"I'm not just a lumberjack, Lerna. I'm also a mountain lion shifter. It's in my blood, and I can't control it."

Lerna's eyes widened in shock. "A shifter? Like... werewolves?"

Baran nodded, relieved that she wasn't running away from him.

"Something like that. But instead of turning into a wolf, I turn into a mountain lion. It's a part of me, and I can't change it."

"That's a good one." She started to laugh and put a hand to his chest. "No, really, what's going on?"

Great, she didn't believe him. Had he expected any different? It sounded like something out of a horror novel.

Lerna looked at Baran's face and searched his expression. Her smile dropped and her hand fell from his chest when she saw he wasn't laughing.

"You're not joking?"

Baran nodded, still feeling uneasy.

"I know it's hard to believe, but it's true. And I wanted to tell you because... because I care about you, Lerna."

Lerna's eyes widened again. "You do?" she asked, surprised.

Baran nodded, his heart racing. "Yes, Lerna. I care about you a lot. You're my fated one."

"Fated one? Wait." She stepped backed a few paces, her hand up to stop him when he started toward her.

Baran ached to pull her back into his arms, but let her have her space.

"You're saying shifters are real? Like really real?"

"Yes. We hide ourselves from the humans."

"Why?"

"Can you imagine what the government would do if they found out about us? Humans, by nature, do not like things they can't understand."

"Can you show me?"

"Are you going to run?"

"I, uh, no. I guess not. This is something I'm going to have to see to believe. You get that right?"

Baran hesitated for a moment before nodding and taking a step back. He pulled off his t-shirt and tossed it to the ground. He kept his eyes locked on Lerna as he toed off his shoes. Her eyes followed his hands as he unbuttoned his pants and lowered the zipper.

"If you want to turn around, you can," he offered. "It's a bitch to shift with clothes on."

"No, I'm okay. Keep going."

The scent of her lust permeated the surrounding air. He dropped his jeans and boxer briefs to the ground and stepped out of them. Eyes closed, he focused on the shift. His body began to contort and stretch, his flesh coated with golden fur.

Lerna took a step back as his form shifted and changed until he stood before her as a massive mountain lion. Her breath caught in her chest, heart pounding out a rapid beat. Her instinct was to run from the dangerous predator a mere foot away from her.

He stayed completely still, as if he knew that any movement would send her running for the hills. His golden coat glistened in the sunlight.

She tentatively reached out a trembling hand and stroked the soft fur on his head. His chest rumbled with her touch, nuzzling into her hand. She ran her hand over his sleek flank and his tail twitched in response. Baran's cat luxuriated in her touch. If he had his way, they'd stay there the rest of the afternoon with her petting him.

Baran shifted back into his human form, and Lerna looked at him in awe and wonder. "That was amazing," she breathed out, still in shock. "I can't believe it."

"I'm sorry if I scared you," Baran said, taking her hand in his. "I just couldn't keep it from you any longer. I wanted you to know who I am and what I'm capable of."

Lerna smiled at him. "I'm not scared. I'm... fascinated," she said.

CHAPTER 13

Lerna couldn't believe what she had seen. A man turning into a mountain lion. It was unbelievable, and yet, she saw it with her own eyes.

"I can't believe this is real. How did you become this way?"

"I was born a shifter. My parents are shifters."

"You weren't bitten or anything?"

Baran shook his head.

"It doesn't work like that. We can't go around changing humans with a bite. The only way a human can change is if they are a true mate of a shifter."

"True mate?"

"The one person fated for you."

Lerna felt a rush of heat go through her body as Baran said those words. She had never believed in fate or destiny, but looking at him, she felt like it all made sense. It was like every puzzle piece in her life had been leading her here, to Baran, to this moment.

"You think I'm your true mate, Baran?" she asked, her voice barely above a whisper.

Baran's eyes widened in surprise, but then a smile spread across his face.

"I know it," he said, pulling her into his arms. "I've known it since the moment I met you."

They stood there, wrapped up in each other, feeling the connection that they couldn't explain. It was like they had known each other for years, even though it had been less than a day.

"What does that mean?"

"It means that we were meant to be together. Our souls are entwined, and we belong to each other," Baran explained, his eyes fixed on hers.

Lerna felt her cheeks heat as she met his intense gaze.

"I don't know what to say," she muttered, feeling a mix of confusion and excitement.

"You don't have to say anything," Baran replied, taking her hand and pulling her closer. "Just feel it."

Lerna's breath caught in her throat as Baran leaned in and pressed his lips to hers. She closed her eyes and melted into the kiss, feeling a rush of desire wash over her. This was what she had been waiting for, even if she didn't know it. They stood there, wrapped up in each other, feeling the connection that she couldn't explain. It was like they had known each other for years, even though it had only been days.

As they broke apart, Lerna looked up at Baran. "What happens now?"

CHAPTER 14

"We keep you safe," Baran ground out. "We can keep you hid and protected."

"We?"

"My crew."

"Are they shifters too?" She looked up at him with wide eyes. The small tendrils of hair framing her face fluttered in the breeze. Baran had forgotten he was still naked until his dick hardened against her thigh, rubbing the soft material of his shorts that she wore. She felt it too as her face turned bright red.

"Let me get my clothes on." He stepped back.

She averted her gaze as he gathered the items. He groaned when he caught her scent again. His shaft throbbed with the need to bury himself inside her sweet pussy. Stepping into his underwear he swore he heard her groan as he bent over. He smiled glad to know he wasn't the only one affected. He drew the material up his legs slowly and let her look her fill.

His cock throbbed as a myriad of emotions flit across her face. He lifted his hand, cupping her jaw. She leaned into him, eyes fluttering shut. His thigh brushed the sweet spot between her legs. She gasped as her drenched pussy fluttered against him. He bit back a groan as she rubbed against him.

No longer able to resist the temptation of her pouty lips, he lowered his mouth to hers. She whimpered as he kissed her. He tasted her mouth, allowing his tongue to part her soft lips. A groan escaped him as she pressed her body closer to his. Deepening the kiss, his tongue brushed hers, allowing her to taste his desire before he pulled away. Her face was flushed, and her eyes were bright with need.

His dick yearned to fill her sweet pussy. He grabbed her hand and led her to the passenger side of the truck. He needed a moment before he lost control and took her on the ground like the animal he turned into. Taking his place on the driver's side, he started the engine. Lerna wound the bottom edge of his shirt around her slim fingers.

"What are you thinking?" Baran asked as he pulled back onto the gravel road.

She threw her head back onto the seat. "How crazy my life has become in the past couple of weeks. How everything has changed. I went from a college student slash waitress to being on the run from my gangster ex-boyfriend and meeting you. And it feels right. Like I'm supposed to be here with you. Like I'm home. It's confusing."

"I'm not going to push you for anything, Lerna. I can't imagine everything that is running through your head. All you need to know is I'll keep you safe." Baran grabbed her hand and twined their fingers. "Everything else will come with time."

"I know. It's scary how much I trust that."

"It's because we're fated."

"What exactly does that mean?"

"You're the one person made for me."

"But how do you know?"

"Your scent."

"You know by the way I smell?"

"As soon as I got close enough to pick up your scent, I knew."

"That sounds crazy, you know."

"A lot of shifters don't believe in a fated mate. It happens very rarely."

"Are there a lot? Shifters I mean," she asked.

"Yes. You've probably met some before and didn't know it. We blend in with humans."

"Are there different shifters?"

"Yes. If you can think of a predatory animal, there's a shifter. We tend to stay in the areas where it's the animal's natural habitat so as not to raise suspicion if a human sees us in our shifted forms."

"Are there a lot of mountain lions around here?"

"Some. Enough that it wouldn't draw attention if someone saw us."

"Do you shift a lot?"

"A few times a month, I let my cat out to run."

"When you're shifted, do you know what you're doing?"

Baran nodded. "It's like we're two halves of a whole. I have a cat's heightened senses when I'm human and the cat has my reasoning, but he's more primal."

"Like hunting?"

"He does like a rabbit every now and then." Baran chuckled and then laughed at the disgusted look on her face.

"Poor bunny."

"It's natural. Survival of the fittest. I promise that there are a lot more rabbits out there than we could eat."

"It's still gross," Lerna stated, her nose wrinkling.

"I'll remind him not to bring you back a gift."

"How does this mating thing work?"

"Umm-"

"Is it a done deal? Do not pass go, do not collect two hundred dollars?"

"No, it's not like that. You have a choice."

"Is there a ceremony?"

"Not really. Some packs have one, but it's just a chance to celebrate a mating. It's not something we just decide to do. It's a lifelong commitment. Once you're mated, that's it."

"No divorce for shifters?"

"No, when we mate, there is a bond that forms between the two. It's hard to explain." He drummed his thumb on the steering wheel.

"What if fate's wrong?"

At her words, Baran felt as if a knife had stabbed him in the chest. Would she deny their bond? The thought never occurred to him.

"I have to trust that fate knows what it's doing."

"If I do say yes, what will happen?"

"We'll spend time together, get to know one another, and make sure that we're compatible."

"What happens if we're not?"

He looked over at her. Her eyes were solemn as she bit her bottom lip.

"There's not a doubt in my mind that we'll be great together. In all ways."

He trailed his finger up her arm, and she shivered, goose-bumps covering her soft skin.

A smile spread across his face.

"That's not what I meant," she huffed out. "Obviously we're attracted to each other."

"Attracted? That's putting it mildly."

"But we're two different people. Species? Hell, I don't even know." Lerna crossed her arms and stared out the window.

"Does it bother you?'" Baran couldn't keep the hurt out of his voice.

"You have to admit, it's a lot for me to swallow."

Baran imagined her swallowing something else. Damn it,

he had to get out of the truck and away from her enticing scent.

"You took it a lot better than I expected, actually."

"I blame it on the paranormal romance novels I've read," she muttered softly.

"Romance novels?"

"They were all wolf shifters. It didn't prepare me for mountain lions."

"What do you want to know? About me or shifters."

"You're born this way, right?"

Baran nodded.

"We get a lot of traits from our animal half. Acute hearing, great sense of smell. We're stronger than humans and we live a lot longer."

"Like you're immortal?"

"No, we're not immortal. It's rare that we get sick and unless we receive a deadly injury like getting our heads chopped off or something else catastrophic, we'll live to a very ripe old age."

"How ripe?"

Baran rubbed a hand across the back of his neck. "A couple of centuries. The oldest living shifter recorded was over two hundred years old."

"Holy shit!" Lerna had a dazed look on her face, as if she couldn't grasp the concept of living over two centuries.

"It's one reason we keep to ourselves. Could you imagine if humans found out? They'd want to dissect us to find out how it's possible."

"They'd see you as the fountain of youth or some kind of miracle cure."

"We'd become some crazy scientist's experiment on how to make humanity better."

"At the cost of your lives. And you can't bite someone and change them?"

"In a roundabout way, that's right."

"What do you mean?"

"We can't go around biting random people and turning them. If that was the case, most of the world's population would be shifters instead of human."

"Would that be a bad thing?"

"There are bad shifters just like there are bad humans. They'd try to take over the world."

"What about human mates? I know you said it's rare, but they have to watch them die at a young age? That's not fair."

"If a shifter's mate is human, they can be changed, but it takes more than a bite."

"What else is there?" She leaned toward him, and he shifted to relieve the pressure on his hard cock.

"Sex," he ground out.

"Excuse me?"

"The couple has sex and when the male comes, he bites his mate. Or she bites him."

"Bites?" She squeaked. "You're going to bite me?!"

"When-If you agree to be my mate, I'll make you feel so good that'll you'll never feel any pain." Baran looked over at her and let her see the lust he felt. Her breath caught.

Fuck, he couldn't get enough of her scent. His cat yowled inside him, wanting her to touch him again.

CHAPTER 15

The heat in Baran's gaze made her shiver. She wanted his hands on her. Could almost feel them. Her nipples pebbled beneath his borrowed shirt.

"You're going to let me choose whether I want to be your mate or not?"

He looked affronted. "Yes, you get a choice! I'm not going to force you into anything. What the hell kind of person do you think I am?"

"I wasn't sure. I'm sorry."

"If you were a shifter, it wouldn't matter. You'd feel the same pull to mate that I do. But you're human. You can't deny that you feel something."

"I can't explain it. It's like I've known you my whole life."

"When two shifters meet their mates, the call is instantaneous. They're usually mated within a few hours, and then figure everything else out."

"What if they're not living in the same place? One of them must give up everything to be with the other one?"

"I'm not saying there aren't challenges, but most shifters believe it's worth it."

"If I asked you to pack up everything and come back with me to Chicago, you would?"

"Yes."

Lerna jerked back at the vehemence in his voice. He really would. Her heart warmed at the thought that he would sacrifice his life here in Texas to be with her.

"Good thing I'm not asking then, huh?"

"Is Chicago where you're from?"

"No, I grew up in Colorado. I'm going to school in Chicago."

"What are you going for?"

"I'm majoring in accounting with a minor in business administration."

"You're good with numbers?"

"Yes. Most people hate math, but I love it. I like it when everything evens out and makes sense."

"What were your plans after school?"

"Nothing specific. Start working at company and get some experience. I toyed with the idea of opening my own accounting firm down the road. Now I'm not sure what's going to happen."

"What do you mean?"

"I left in the middle of the term. I've missed several tests. I'm probably failing all my classes now." Her head fell back against the seat. All her hard work would have been for nothing. She'd be out of the money for her tuition and books and have to take the classes over again.

"Can you let them know that you had an emergency? See if you can catch up later?"

"I'm scared. What if they track where I sent the email from? Enzo has some smart people working with him and they aren't afraid to break the law to get what they want."

"Is that why you didn't go to the police?"

"He told me he had some of the police force in his pocket. What if I told the wrong person?"

"He already knows where you are in a roundabout way. Email your professors and see if they'll give you an extension. We'll drive a couple of hours away and use some random internet. I'm betting you've been a model student and never missed a class. They're probably worried about you."

"No, I never miss class."

"What about your family?"

"I spoke with my sister right before they caught me in Dallas. If I don't get in touch with her soon, she'll be on a plane to Texas."

"What about your parents?"

"They're on an Alaskan cruise and won't be back for a few more days."

"We'll need to get you a disposable phone to call them and let them know you're okay."

"Then what? I hide out in your trailer? What if they track you down? Got your license plate number the other night?" Her voice became higher pitched with every question.

"Slow down before you get all worked up. You're staying with me as long as you want. If they track the plate number, it'll take them time to figure out where we are. It's registered to my work address. I doubt they got it, though. It was dark, and they were more worried about shooting at us."

"Don't remind me," she groaned out.

Baran flipped the lever for the blinker, and they turned into the RV park. They passed several types of RVs and campers. Some were plain and older, some brand new and fancy with slides. One of them looked bigger than her apartment back in Chicago.

"Why do some of them have porches? Do they live here?"

"It's cheap. Water and electricity are included in the rent. Some people live here full time. Some come on the weekends. There's a lake a few miles down the road that is popular in the summer. They'll keep their boats docked there."

"Do you all stay here?"

"Yes. We bring three with us when we travel and share. Vonn and I stay together. The others decided who is staying where."

Baran pointed to an RV. "That one is ours and the one next to it."

Lerna looked them over as they drove past. They weren't new, but seemed to be in good shape. A burgundy canopy shaded the door and a pair of camp chairs leaned up against the side. A black smoker puffed out gray smoke from the stack. Adirondack chairs ringed a brick fire pit. The empty area to the right of the second trailer had a volleyball net erected. A tall blonde woman waved as they passed by.

"That's Holland. She recently came to work with us."

"Is she a shifter too?"

"We all are. Her father is the alpha and had ordered her to mate with a male from another pride. She refused and left."

"He ordered her?" she asked in horror.

"Shifters are like natural packs and prides. There is a hierarchy. The alpha rules the pack."

"It sucks anyway you look at it. We're not in the Middle Ages."

"I agree."

"Who's the Alpha of your group?"

"You're looking at him." His mouth kicked up into a grin.

"Really? You run your pack?"

"Yes."

"How does that work? You order everyone around?"

"There's more to it than that."

"Does that mean you're the biggest and the strongest?"

"I'm not the biggest, but I am the strongest. That's not all it takes to be an alpha. I keep my people safe and lead them. They're more important than me. Any decision I make has to benefit the whole pride. Not just one person."

They turned into the small parking spot across from

Baran's trailer. Vonn was still sitting in a chair with his legs propped up on the table.

"Vonn's my Beta. He's in charge if I'm not around."

"You're all mountain lions?"

"We're a little different. We have a few different cat breeds. Some shifters won't allow different breeds to join their prides, but I'm not that way."

As they approached, Vonn straightened up, tipping up the brim of his cap. "Guys decided we're having a cookout tonight. Might be a good time to have Lerna meet everyone."

"That's a good idea. She needs to know who she can trust. Saw those two assholes that nabbed her over in Collins."

Vonn's amiable smile fell from his face. "And you didn't go after them?"

"No, Lerna didn't want us to get wrapped up in it."

"That's horseshit," Vonn spat out. "Pardon my French. Have you told her?"

Baran looked down at Lerna and squeezed her hand. "She knows."

"Good. Did you get their scent?"

"No, the windows were up and there were a lot of people. Unless I was right up on them, I wouldn't have been able to decipher their scents."

"Damn. That would have been helpful."

"Lerna, why don't you on into the trailer? I'll join you in a minute."

"Sure." Lerna looked at Baran and then Vonn.

Vonn opened the door and ushered her inside.

"What's the plan?" Vonn asked as he shut the door.

"Keep her safe. These assholes have everything to lose if she's able to tell what she saw."

"And that was?"

"They killed a man. She was hiding in the bedroom but saw it."

"Why not go to the cops?"

"His family is a big deal. Bribed some of the force. She didn't know who she could trust."

"Poor girl. What do you want us to do?"

"Keep an eye out for any strangers. We know who hangs around these parts. They aren't going to blend in too well. She can get to know everyone today."

"How long are you thinking?"

"As long as it takes. I'll do whatever it takes to keep her safe."

"And after that?"

"That'll be up to her. I can't force her to choose me and stay. She has a life up north."

"Didn't you explain it to her? What being your fated mate means?"

"Some of it. Not all. I didn't want to influence her decision."

"Must suck to be stuck with a human." Vonn shook his head. "If she was a shifter, it wouldn't be a question."

"Watch your mouth," Baran growled. "She's my mate, and she's perfect. None of you will say a damn word about her being human. If you do, I'll meet you in the pit."

Vonn's head bowed in deference to his Alpha's anger.

"I'm sorry, Alpha. It won't happen again."

CHAPTER 16

Lerna sagged against the door as Baran snapped at Vonn. The air seemed to thicken with his words. She wanted to drop to her knees in supplication.

What hadn't Baran told her? Vonn's tone of voice made it sound serious. As Vonn apologized, the air lightened and she felt as though she could breathe again. She straightened from the door and walked over to the bedroom. Dropping the bags on the unmade bed, she contemplated her next moves.

She needed to contact the school. Baran was right. Her hard work shouldn't go to waste because of that asshole Angelo. Ronnie was first on the list though. She needed to let her sister know she was okay before she called out the National Guard to check on her. The thought of her sister worrying made Lerna sick to her stomach.

On the table was a cell phone. She bit her thumb, debating. If she made a quick call to let Ronnie know she was okay, wouldn't hurt anything, right? She walked over and picked it up. The metal was cool in her hand. She pushed the button on the side and the screen turned on. Swiping her thumb up, she expected the functions to be locked, but was surprised when it opened with any further prompting.

Screw it, she thought.

Her fingers touched the numbers. After two rings, her sister answered.

"Hello?"

"Hey, it's me."

"Oh, thank God," Ronnie breathed out.

"I can't talk long. I wanted you to know I'm safe."

"What the hell happened?" she demanded.

"Angelo found me, but I got away. A guy saved me. That's all I can say for now. I'll call you as soon as I can."

She touched the button to end the call as her sister yelled she better not hang up.

Had she done the right thing?

The phone lit up as her sister called back.

"Is that my phone?" Vonn asked as he came up behind her.

Lerna screamed in surprise, fumbling with the phone and dropping it. Vonn caught it before it hit the floor.

"Shit. Sorry. I didn't mean to scare you."

"You and your damn brother are too quiet. I need to put a bell on you."

"Who did you call?" Vonn asked, slipping the phone into the back pocket of his jeans.

"My sister. She told me if I didn't check in, she'd get law enforcement involved."

"Older sister?"

"Yes."

"She's probably bossy like Baran, too. It's the bane of being the younger sibling."

"Bossy doesn't begin to describe it," Lerna complained. "Where's Baran?"

"He went to check in with the others. He said y'all were going out again to get a phone and let your school know about a family emergency. He wanted to see if y'all needed to pick up anything for tonight."

"Oh," she mumbled.

"Have a seat," he motioned to the banquet set. "Let's talk."

Lerna slide under the table, as did Vonn on the opposite side.

"I know that Baran told you what we are and who you are to him."

"Yeah. I mean, I'm shocked and a little weirded out, but it's fine."

"Weirded out a little?" Vonn asked.

"Okay, a lot. I never would have believed him if he hadn't changed in front of me."

"What did he tell you about mating?"

Lerna squirmed in her seat.

"Let me tell you a little of our history. A long time ago, mates were easy to find. Our prides and packs stayed to themselves and away from humans. They would travel every year to a festival of sorts and meet others. It was more common for us to find our fated one than not."

"What changed?" Lerna leaned forward, placing her elbows on the tabletop. Vonn's voice was almost hypnotic.

"The world's population exploded. Prides and packs scattered further apart. They had to intermingle with humans more. Over the decades, fewer shifters were finding their fated mate. Nowadays, it's rare to find them."

"But you still mate?"

"We're able to love others and create a bond like humans do. It's not as strong as it would be with our fated one, but we can be happy, have a family and live fulfilling lives."

"What hasn't he told me, Vonn?"

"Heard that, huh?" Vonn rubbed a hand across the back of his neck with a wince.

"I may not have your super hearing, but I was still at the door."

"Shit. He'll kill me, but I think you need to know all of it."

"Then tell me."

"Once you've met your fated mate, that's it. That's your one shot. With shifters, it's a no brainer. But with you being human, you don't feel the connection."

"What are you saying?"

"If you turn Baran down, he'll never have another chance at loving someone."

"But he doesn't love me," she squealed.

"Yet." He pointed at her. "I guarantee he's halfway there."

"That's not possible. It hasn't even been twenty-four hours!"

"You don't believe in love at first sight?"

"Lust yes. Love no."

"You admit you're lusting after him." Vonn waggled his eyebrows and smirked.

"Oh, good grief." Lerna flopped back against the cushion. "Yes, I'm attracted to Baran. Who wouldn't be? He's hot."

"Let me ask you a question. If the circumstances were different, if you weren't on the run from a murderous ex, do you think you would have taken the news of shifters so well? Not freaked out when he shifted in front of you?"

"Well," Lerna trailed off.

"You would've laughed in his face when he told you about being a shifter and ran screaming when he shifted. That would be a normal response."

Lerna's mouth snapped shut.

"You feel the connection. Not like he does, but on some level. You know that he's special to you."

"Maybe I'm more open-minded than most humans," she argued.

Vonn cocked an eyebrow.

"Fine," she breathed out. "There is something there. I don't know how to explain it."

"It's like a tether. A beam of light that connects you. The longer you're around each other, the stronger the light becomes, the tether strengthens." Vonn got a far off look in his eyes.

Lerna reached over and covered his hand with hers.

"You've met yours, haven't you?"

"Yes, but it's complicated."

"Is she human too?"

"No, she's a shifter."

"Then what's the problem? I thought it was easer that way."

"Did Baran explain how we know our mates?" He didn't wait for her to answer and plowed on. "It's a scent. I'm different from other shifters. A freak."

"Don't call yourself that!" Lerna snapped.

"Sorry." He gave her a small smile. "I can hide my scent from others. I don't even realize I do it most of the time."

"She doesn't know?"

Vonn shook his head.

"Why not? I mean, you can unhide your scent, right?"

"Yes. I can even choose which scent. She knows I'm a shifter, but not her mate."

"Why are you hiding it?"

"Like I said, it's complicated."

"Then uncomplicate it."

"Easier said than done. She's been through a rough patch."

"Wait, is this who Baran was talking about? The one whose father tried to force her to mate with someone?"

"Holland, yeah."

"And that left a bad taste in her mouth about mating I'm guessing."

Vonn nodded, a frown on his handsome face.

"When she came here, she got shitfaced drunk. She went on and on about how she never wanted to mate, and men were pigs, yada yada."

"You can't blame the girl, but you can't take everything

she said to heart when she was drunk. It was probably the first time she could vent how she felt."

"Maybe," he hedged.

"The tether is getting stronger for you, but not her? What happens the longer you go without telling her?"

"To her, nothing. If I wait long enough, it's not good."

"Tell me," Lerna demanded.

"The pull to be with your mate grows until you can't stand to be apart from them. You become obsessive. Males will become more aggressive toward unmated males around her. She becomes his focus and nothing else matters."

"And if she rejects him?"

"He'll go insane and be put down."

Lerna sat there in shock as the door flew open.

"God damn it Vonn!" Baran roared.

Vonn shifted his eyes from Lerna to his brother.

"What? She asked what would happen if Holland rejected me."

"You son of a bitch," Baran bit out. His chest heaved with his anger, nostrils flaring with each breath.

Vonn met his gaze head on for a second before dropping his eyes to the table.

"Vonn, could you excuse us for a second?" Lerna asked, her focus on Baran. "We need to talk."

"Sure. I'll go see if anyone needs anything."

"Creed and Jasper are unloading the truck. They could use some help."

Vonn stood and squeezed past Baran. The door shut behind him with a click.

CHAPTER 17

"Don't be mad at your brother. I asked him," Lerna begged.

"I'm not mad but, fuck, I don't know. I wanted to be the one to tell you," he breathed out.

"Why didn't you?"

Baran dropped his gaze and ran a hand over his hair.

"I wanted you to make your own choice, not just take a gamble. To choose to be with me out of desire, not fear of the alternative. I wanted you to have the courage to decide for yourself, without any regret or hesitation."

Lerna melted at his words. He reached up and rubbed his hand on the left side of his chest. She felt an answering flutter on hers. Was this the tether that Vonn had spoken of? She slid out of the banquet and stood beside him. Baran gazed down at her, eyes full of hope, worry and, dare she dream, love?

She placed her hands on his chest. His heart thumped against her palm. Strong and steady, like the man. Upwards, her hands traveled until she reached his face. His beard brushed against her palms, and she couldn't wait to feel it rubbing on other parts of her skin.

He cupped the sides of her waist with his large hands and drew her closer until her breasts were cushioned against him.

"Lerna," he breathed out, lowering his head.

She raised up to meet his lips. At the mere touch, her body lit up as if touching a live wire. His hand rose, cupping the back of her neck, pulling her tighter into the kiss. His warm tongue breached her lips and danced along hers. Lerna felt as if she couldn't get close enough to Baran. She whimpered with need.

Baran bent his knees and put his arm under her ass, lifting her. Her legs wrapped around his waist. He stepped into his bedroom and placed her on the bed, his lips never leaving hers. He moved over her, pinning her to the bed. The weight of his body on hers filled Lerna with liquid heat.

His hands traveled down her body, skimming over her curves and sending sparks of electricity through her.

Baran broke off the kiss and pulled back. His eyes were a blazing gold.

"As good as you look in my clothes, I want them off," he growled. Lerna gasped as he tore her clothing from her body.

He quickly shed his shirt.

She traced his torso with her fingers, kneading his chest and letting her nails scratch along the hairs. He jerked in her embrace and laid her on the bed. His gaze roamed her body, lingering on the junction of her thighs. She felt hot under his perusal and didn't hide her nakedness. Her breasts rose and fell with each quickened breath.

Lerna reached for the button on his jeans and opened them. He hissed as the zipper slid down. She pushed his jeans and briefs down in one go. Her breath caught at the sight of his cock. It was long and thick. Veins stood out under the skin. She couldn't wait to feel it inside her. She reached out her hand, but he grabbed hold of her wrist.

"Are you sure, Lerna?"

His eyes searched her face.

"Yes," she uttered in desperation. She felt as if her body would go up in flames if he stopped touching her. A rumble escaped his throat. He shook his head.

"What is it?"

"My cat is trying to come forth." He pulled back. "I don't want to hurt you."

"I don't care if you do," she admitted. "I want you. All of you."

She reached for him again. He didn't stop her this time. She took him in her palm and stroked up and down. He shuddered under her touch. His cock was warm and smooth in her hand. She pumped harder and applied more pressure. Pleasure and need coiled in her belly. She needed Baran inside her.

"Fuck!" he cursed.

She pumped her hand a few more times before sitting up and grasping the base of his shaft. She leaned forward and licked the tip of him. He tasted salty. She slid her lips over the head and moaned. Baran's breath hissed through his teeth. Lerna tightened her grip on his cock. She felt it pulse under her fingers. She opened her mouth and slid down further, taking more and more of him. The tip hit the back of her throat. She slowly pulled back until only the head was inside and then repeated the motion.

She glanced up to see his eyes closed with a look of bliss on his face. He reached out and grabbed her wrist.

"Enough," he growled.

"But-"

"If you keep that up, I'll come before I get inside that sweet pussy of yours."

He let go of her wrist and feathered a kiss on her mouth. He nibbled down her neck. They sucked and bit at each other's skin, need driving them.

His hands pulled her up to a sitting position. Lerna reached out for him, but he stopped her hand. Baran lowered himself to his knees and laved his tongue over one nipple, then the next. Her back arched in response. Her fingers curled into the bedding as his tongue circled and flicked her nipples.

Her fingers combed through his hair. A deep growl rumbled in Baran's chest, and he nipped at her breast, making her yelp.

"I'm not going to hurt you, but I'm going to take my time to worship your body. Learn everything that makes you whimper and moan."

Hearing his words made Lerna tremble.

He lowered himself and continued his sensual assault on her sensitive breasts. His left hand rose and cupped her left breast. His right hand slid down her body and rested on her thigh. He caressed her belly with his hand, moving lower. Lerna moaned as his hand reached her core. His thumb caressed the sensitive nub of her clit, and she jerked in his arms.

He kissed his way down her stomach. His hands parted her thighs and his head lowered to her pussy. He licked and nibbled at her right thigh, his eyes never leaving hers. His tongue moved higher, caressing the crease of her thigh and hip. She knew he was sneaking a glance at her pussy, but she couldn't muster any embarrassment. She was too far gone.

He licked up and down her slit. His tongue was hot and wet against her. He laved her pussy, alternating between fast and slow strokes. Her body vibrated with the need to orgasm. She moaned and gasped, clutching her hands in his hair. The pleasure was too much to bear. Her entire body felt as if it was on fire.

Baran's tongue swirled around her clit, and then he sucked on it. She cried out with the intense pleasure. His mouth became relentless. He stuck his tongue inside her and flicked it against her walls. She arched into him, needing more. He groaned and licked her hungrily. Her hips bucked, and she whimpered. Baran growled and a rush of liquid heat shot through her.

She moaned his name as the orgasm ripped through her. Baran held her hips still as he continued his sexual ministrations. Lerna's hips moved of their own accord, desperate for more.

"Please," she moaned.

He plunged his tongue into her, and she felt another orgasm threaten. Her clit swelled under his ministrations. Baran continued his assault until she was begging for release.

"Please," she moaned.

His tongue slid over her clit, drawing it into his mouth while thrusting a finger into her core. Her mind exploded. She felt as if she was spinning out of control as pleasure consumed her.

She cried out as the orgasm rushed through her. Her hands dug into his shoulders as her world shattered as she jerked in his arms. Her muscles tensed and released as wave after wave of ecstasy encompassed her.

She collapsed on the bed, chest heaving. Lerna watched as he licked his lips, eyes shining gold. He crawled up her body, settling between the juncture of her thighs.

He held her gaze as he pushed his cock inside her. Her pussy gripped him like a hot, wet fist. The need to cum boiled up. He bit back a growl.

"Baran," she panted.

"You're so tight," he murmured.

His cock filled her to the point it was almost too much. He rotated his hips, pressing his pelvis against her clit. Sparks of pleasure went off inside her. She needed him to move. To do something.

"Please," she whimpered.

His smile was wicked as he retreated and slammed back into her. Her thighs tightened around his hips. Slow retreat and deep hard thrust. He kept this pace until she writhed beneath him. He placed his thumb on her clit and rubbed in time to his thrusts. Her climax built in her core, but she needed more.

"Baran," she begged.

He lowered his arms on each side of her head, bending her legs toward the outside of her chest. He kissed her lips tenderly.

"I wanted to take this slow, draw it out, but you feel too good. You're burning me up."

His words caused streaks of heat to race through her core. He pushed into her hard and fast. She felt every ridge of his cock as he slid in and out of her. She moved her head to the side and bit his arm to hold back her scream of pleasure. Baran grunted and quickened his pace. His cock plunged into her with swift thrusts. She could feel the head of him push against her womb. Her breathing came in gasps. His hands gripped her thighs, and he lowered his head and pressed his lips to hers. She could taste herself on his tongue. The sensation of his cock thrusting into her and his tongue in her mouth was intoxicating.

Beads of sweat dripped from his forehead onto her breasts. His breathing was as ragged as hers. The sound grew louder in her ears and the world seemed to spin as Baran slammed into her, his strokes long and hard. His cock hit spots inside of her she never knew existed. She jerked as he slammed into her, sending her over the edge. Her fingers flexed and clawed at his back. She clung to him as her body shook, moaning his name.

She felt his cock jerk inside her, flooding her with more heat. He lifted his head and roared at the ceiling before collapsing beside her. He buried his face in her neck and panted. Kissing her neck, he moved up to her lips. He sucked at her bottom lip. Her body throbbed around his cock.

"That was incredible," she whispered.

"Yes, it was, but it's not over yet," he whispered. He drew

back his still rock-hard shaft. Their combined releases coated her thighs.

His teeth bit down on her nipple, and she arched into him. He licked away the sting. He turned her over onto her stomach. She felt him move between her legs as he pulled her up onto her hands and knees. His cock nudge at the entrance to her wet pussy. She spread her legs wider. Baran gripped her ass in his hands. Lerna screamed as he impaled her with a hard thrust. She lowered her chest to the bed, arching her ass in supplication.

His hand slid over her back and grasped her shoulder, holding her in place. His other hand reached under and rubbed her clit. He worked her body like a well-oiled machine. He pumped into her faster. Lerna's body was on fire with the need to climax again. She pushed back against him, meeting his thrusts.

Baran's breathing grew ragged. His chest blanketed her back. She felt his mouth at her shoulder, teeth pressing into her flesh. The pain set off her orgasm as she exploded, milking his cock. His head turned to the side as he continued to thrust into her, as his cock jerked inside her.

She moaned as his release drew out her orgasm. His head rested on her shoulder as he pressed a kiss to the place he'd bitten. She felt him ease out of her. She collapsed on her stomach, panting for breath. He gently turned her over until she was on her back. Baran smiled at her and brushed the hair off her face.

"I never knew it could be like that," she whispered.

"Me either."

CHAPTER 18

The evening air had cooled enough that the fire the men had blazing was a comfort. Earlier, Baran had taken her into town so she could get a burner phone and email her professors about her supposed family emergency. She felt enough relief that she could relax for the first time in days and enjoy the company of Baran's pride.

Lerna leaned back in her lawn chair and sipped the beer Creed had handed her earlier. Warmth radiated through her body, and she felt relaxed. She watched as Baran and Creed talked and laughed with one another. Baran looked over at her with a smile as he talked and his eyes softened when he saw her watching him, and he winked at her before turning back to his conversation. Lerna couldn't help but smile to herself as she took another sip of beer.

"Looks like that cold front they've been predicting is finally hitting," Jasper remarked from his seat.

"How can you tell?" Lerna asked.

"Just can," he answered.

"Don't expect a lot of talk from Jasper. He's the strong quiet type," Holly quipped.

Jasper shot her the finger.

"We can tell a difference in the air. It'll storm tonight and we'll finally get a break from this dreadful heat," he said before joining the other men.

"I can't believe how hot it is here in October," Lerna added.

"I know. Where I'm from, it's already chilly and the mountains are starting to get snow," Holly added.

"Where are you from?"

"Colorado. You?"

"Me too," Lerna answered with surprise. "What part?"

"About fifty miles north of Denver. A little town called Cabot Springs. I thought Baran said you're from Chicago."

"I'm going to school there, but I was born and raised in Colorado Springs. It's a small world, isn't it?"

"Sure is. You and Baran are mates, huh?"

"That's what he says."

"You don't believe him?" Holly cocked an eyebrow.

"I don't know what to believe. Something inside of me wants to accept his words as truth, but I'm torn. I know that what I feel for him is nothing I've ever felt before. And after everything I've witnessed lately, I'm willing to trust what he says."

Holly laughed. "I can only imagine."

"I hope you don't mind, but Baran told me why you joined his pride."

The smile dropped from Holly's face.

"My dad's an asshole," she remarked.

"I agree. It took a lot of guts to leave your family."

"I would've left them if I had agreed to the mating. Jeff was from another pride in North Dakota. It was to make the alliance between our prides stronger."

"Your dad sounds like a dick," Lerna blurted out.

"He is. He's very old-fashioned. Females are to be seen and not heard and obey the males of the pride."

"Was it your dad or the mating you were against?"

"Both. It may have been different if Jeff was a nice guy, but he's a bully. I wasn't going to spend my life with someone like him."

"What about if you find your mate like Baran did?"

"My fated mate?"

"Yes," answered Lerna as she looked across the fire to where Vonn was staring at them both.

"I don't know. My dad told me that there is no such thing as a fated mate. That it was an old wives' tale. My mom always believed that a mate was something you were born with and that it's more than physical attraction. It's not even the same as love at first sight. There's a pull, a need when you meet them that leaves you breathless. Which one is telling the truth?" Holly shrugged. "No one in my pride has a fated mate."

"My mom used to moon about my dad being her soul mate. It made me and my sister gag as they'd make goo-goo eyes at each other. After meeting Baran, I'm beginning to believe that souls mates or fated mates, whatever you call them, are real."

Holly smiled. "I hope it's true, but I'm not getting my hopes up. It's a million in one shot to find that person meant for you."

"I wouldn't bet on that," Lerna quipped and looked at Vonn.

The smile on his face confirmed that with his superior hearing, he had heard her words.

Holly's eyes followed hers. The heated look that passed between the two made Lerna want to fan herself to cool off. When Vonn winked at her, Holly ducked her head and blushed. Lerna couldn't wait for the sparks to fly when they finally realized what they meant to each other.

Holly tucked her loose blonde hair behind her ear and caught Lerna looking at her.

"What?"

"Nothing," Lerna grinned.

"It's not like Vonn is my mate. I've been around him long enough to know."

"Maybe you need to speak with Vonn about that," Lerna hedged. She didn't want to reveal Vonn's secret.

"What am I missing?"

"Talk to Vonn."

"But-"

A truck slid to a stop next to the trailer, cutting off Holly. An older gentleman jumped out of the driver's seat and hustled over to where Baran stood. After a few words, Baran's eyes flew to Lerna's. She stood from her chair, dread filling her. Her stomach churned and bile rose.

"What's going on?" she whispered to Holly.

"That's Tarek. He went over to the Watering Hole earlier. He said that he saw some guys he didn't recognize, and they were asking about Baran's truck."

"Oh fuck," Lerna breathed out. "I've got to get out of here."

"Not so fast. You're one of us now. We'll keep you safe. Trust us. Trust Baran."

"But I'm not one of you."

"You may not have mated Baran yet but, that doesn't change anything. He said you're his mate, and that's all it took. Bite or no bite."

Lerna touched the place on the back of her shoulder that Baran had bitten earlier. He'd assured her he hadn't broken the skin, binding her to him.

Baran looked over at Creed and Jasper and barked out a few harsh words. They bolted for the truck with Tarek in hot pursuit. Baran held Lerna's gaze as he walked forward.

"Lerna," he started.

"I need to leave, Baran. I can't put you guys in danger."

"No," he barked out. "You're not leaving. They're too close."

"What is the Watering Hole? Holly said that was where Tarek saw them."

"It's a dive bar we go to blow off some steam after work. It's only a few miles down the road."

"They're way too close."

Lerna turned to walk away and Baran grabbed her arm gently, aware of his greater strength.

"Creed, Jasper, and Tarek are headed back there to keep an eye on them. We're going to come up with a plan."

"These guys are killers, Baran. I couldn't stand it if any of you were hurt, or God forbid, killed because of me."

"You're forgetting that we're shifters. It's hard as hell to kill us."

"That's not the point, Baran! I don't want you to get hurt because of me," she cried.

Baran stopped in front of her and cupped her cheeks.

"I won't let you go," he murmured.

Baran's face blurred before her eyes, and then the floodgates opened. Before she knew what was happening, Lerna was in his arms, sobbing heartbrokenly.

"Lerna," he whispered in her ear. "I won't let anything happen to you, I promise."

Lerna clung to Baran as he led her to a chair and sat down next to her. She hiccupped and tried to hold back her tears.

"This doesn't change anything."

"Of course it doesn't. I'm your mate. That's all that matters."

"But I'm not strong like you and your friends," she said through her tears.

"It doesn't matter if you're not a warrior or a fighter. You're my mate and I'll protect. You're my responsibility."

"I don't want that. To sit back and have you risk your life because you think I'm your mate."

Lightning fast, he grabbed her around the waist and pulled her to him. "My only concern is keeping you safe."

"How? They have guns, Baran."

"You let me worry about that. I have a plan."

"What plan?"

"I'm going to give them a reason to go after me instead of you."

"Seriously? You're putting a target on your back?" Lerna threw up her hands in frustration. "That's not what I want."

"Too damn bad."

"God save me from stupid men," Lerna uttered. "What if they don't fall for it? Go after your pride instead? What happens when they get in the crossfire?"

"They'll be fine," he consoled her.

"You don't know that. You're not God!" Baran grasped her hands in his and squeezed.

"Lerna, listen to me. We're not human, and we don't play by human rules. You need to trust me. Can you do that?"

Lerna felt in her heart that he meant those words.

"If something bad happens-"

"It won't. I promise you."

"You think your plan is going to work?"

"It will. I'll make them believe they have a chance to take me down and when they do, they'll think they've won until it's too late."

"I don't like this," Lerna said, looking up at him with narrowed eyes.

"I don't either, but we have to get them off your trail. Do you know what it would do to me if I lost you?"

Baran crushed her to his chest. She felt safe wrapped in his powerful arms. She closed her eyes and let the steady rhythm of his heart calm her.

"I can't lose you," he whispered so softly that she struggled to hear the words.

Gravel crunched under a shoe. Lerna looked over to see Holly and Vonn standing beside them.

"What's the plan?"

CHAPTER 19

"I'm heading up to the cabin at the lake. Creed and Jasper are going to let it slip that they've seen my truck and where to find me."

"We're setting a trap?" Vonn asked.

"We'll surround them when they get to the cabin and take them down."

"And then what?" Lerna inquired. "You can't just turn them over to the police."

"They've messed with a shifter's mate. That falls under shifter law. We'll deal with them," Vonn stated.

"Shifter law? What the hell is that?"

"It means when our mates are threatened, we can do whatever it takes to make sure they are safe." Vonn said.

Lerna paled at the deadly tone he had taken.

"What about me? Where am I going to be?" Lerna asked Baran.

"You'll stay here with Holly where it's safe."

"Oh, screw that," Lerna fumed, pushing away from Baran.

"I don't want to be left out either," Holly added.

"No," Baran said firmly.

"If you're going, I want to be by your side," Lerna snapped back at him.

Baran opened his mouth to respond, but then closed it again. His jaw tightened.

"Lerna."

"I'm going to stay in the cabin with her," Holly added. "You didn't think I'd let you go alone, did you?"

"God save me from stubborn females," Baran uttered, looking heavenward.

"This is my fight, Baran." Lerna pointed her finger at him. "I'm not going to sit back like a damsel in distress and let you fight my battles for me."

"I need you to be safe," Baran argued.

"Holly can stay inside the cabin with me. I won't go outside. I can't be left out. I need to be there," Lerna pleaded.

Baran saw Lerna was serious. It went against every instinct he possessed to let her willingly go into danger.

"If you don't let them, they'll sneak out and follow us," Vonn whispered to him.

Holly smirked.

"Fine," Baran breathed out. He looked at Lerna. "You stay in the cabin. You don't come out for any reason. I can't be worrying about you and do what I need to do."

Lerna nodded. Baran turned his gaze to Holly.

"You will guard her with your life."

"Yes, Alpha. No one will touch her."

"I can't believe I'm agreeing to this," he muttered. "Pack some things and let's go."

CHAPTER 20

"Where are we going?" Lerna asked from beside Baran. Her fingers drummed on the console between them. He reached over and covered her hand with his.

"The pride owns a cabin on the lake a few miles from here. It's been in the pride for a few generations."

The night was clear, with thousands of twinkling lights dotting the inky blackness above them and the moon high in the sky. The water was a dark, glistening black, like the night sky, but reflected in the water's surface. A cabin loomed before them, silhouetted against the moonlit water. Lerna shivered as the memories of old horror movies flashed in her brain. The ones her sister made her watch so she could scare the hell out of her at the right time. Lerna smiled at the memory of the time she tossed a bowl of popcorn into the air when her sister goosed her at one of the jump scares. She hoped she'd get to see her sister again.

"Stop," Baran whispered.

"What?" Lerna asked as she turned to him. The moonlight silhouetted half of his face, but his eyes had that eerie golden glow.

Maybe monsters were real, she thought.

"Stop thinking whatever put that frown on your face. It's going to be all right."

"You don't know that," Lerna countered, looking down at her clasped hands.

"I promise that I will do everything in my power to keep you safe," Baran vowed.

"Me too," Vonn chimed in.

"And me," Holly added.

"You're part of our pride." Baran placed a finger under her chin, and she lifted her eyes to his. "We will die for you."

Lerna's chin trembled as she fought back the tears. He meant what he said. They would die for her.

"I pray it doesn't come to that."

"Me either."

The nature sounds of crickets and frogs filled the night as Baran led Lerna out of the truck. Crisp air pebbled the skin of Lerna's arms as she rubbed her hands up and down them to warm them up.

"Vonn, get the generator up and running," Baran ordered as he picked up their bags from the bed of the truck.

"On it," Vonn replied, taking off at a jog around the back-side of the cabin.

As they ascended the sturdy wooden steps, a motor roared to life in the distance. The front porch lights flared to life, illuminating the wide porch, eliminating the *Chainsaw Massacre* effect to *Better Homes and Gardens*. The wooden screen door creaked as Holly pulled it open, but the solid wooden door swung open on silent hinges. She flipped the light switch and illuminated the living room. A large, tan leather couch dominated the room, with a couple of recliners flanking each end. The opposite end of the room held an enormous fireplace surrounded by river rocks.

"This is not what I was expecting," Lerna murmured as she looked around.

"What did you expect?" Baran asked, coming up behind her.

"One room and an outhouse out back," Lerna teased.

"We're a little more civilized than that. I want a working toilet." Baran smiled. "We can rough it if we have to, but I'd rather not. Holly, can you handle getting a fire going? I'll take Lerna to her room."

"Got it, Boss."

Baran turned and proceeded up the wide staircase. At the top of the landing were several doors lining the hallway. Baran passed each closed door and headed for a set of double doors at the far end of the hall. The doors opened and revealed a large room dominated by a four-poster bed. Baran dropped her bag on the bench at the end. Moonlight streamed through the sheer white curtains, giving the room an ethereal glow.

"This is beautiful," Lerna whispered, her gaze moving about the room.

A whoosh from her right drew her attention. Fire flared to life inside the fireplace.

"I'm glad you like it," Baran said, coming up behind her and placing his hands on her shoulders. She leaned back into his chest.

"Bathroom is through that door. There's a nice big tub in there for you to soak in. Try to relax."

"Easier said than done."

"I know." He kissed the top of her head. "But try for me."

"Fine," Lerna huffed out.

He opened the door and ushered her into the enormous bathroom. He was right about the tub. She could submerge herself in it if she wanted. Baran turned on the tap and let the water start to fill it.

"There's plenty of hot water. I'm not sure if there's any stuff to put in the water besides maybe some Epson salt."

"That's fine."

He reached into a cabinet and pulled out a white, fluffy towel.

"There's a robe on the back of the door. I'll bring the rest of the bags up to the room. If you need anything, yell."

As he turned and walked out, she hesitated a moment before blurting out. "What if I need you?"

His hand froze on the door. Looking at her over his shoulder, his eyes blazed gold.

"You'll have me," he growled.

He strode back toward, reminding her of a predator stalking its prey. A shiver coursed over her body. Not one of fear, but anticipation. He grasped her chin, his golden eyes locking onto hers. Lerna's heart raced as she felt the intensity of his gaze, a mix of protectiveness and something more primal stirring within him. Baran leaned in, his breath warm against her lips, before capturing them in a searing kiss. His hands traveled down her torso until it reached the hem of her shirt. They skimmed back up, bringing the material with them. His lips left hers long enough to remove the shirt before he was back to eating at her mouth. Her jeans came loose, and he skimmed them and her underwear down her legs. He trailed his lips down her torso and he knelt.

"Step out," he ordered.

She did as he said, leaving the clothing in a pile on the tiled floor. He buried his face against her mound.

"Fuck, you smell delicious," he moaned, hands gripping her thighs. "Spread them."

Her face flushed hot.

"Now, mate," he growled, thumbs tracing the inside of her thighs.

She placed her feet wide, and he buried his face in her mound. His tongue lapped at her folds as she grasped his head. Hands higher on her thighs, he moved his thumbs to hold her folds open, allowing him more access to the flesh he craved. She groaned, her hips bucking forward as his tongue danced over her clit, sending waves of bliss coursing through her body. Baran continued, his tongue working its magic, making her moan and writhe beneath him. He needed to taste her more, to engorge himself in her taste.

As she came undone, Baran pulled back, lapping at her sensitive flesh before standing. Her knees gave way, and he pulled her to him. She glanced over his shoulder.

"Baran, the tub," she muttered.

"Huh? Oh shit."

Turning to the tub, he saw the water pooling precariously at the rim of the cast iron tub. He shut off the water and faced her again. Lust shone in her eyes. Gripping the hem of his t-shirt, he whipped it over his head. Her hooded gaze followed the movement, her pink tongue emerged, wetting her bottom lip. Her breath hitched when he popped the button on his jeans and let them drop to the floor. His hardened shaft bounced when released from the confines of the denim and her eyes tracked the movement. He heard her heart started pound as her breath quickened. As he stood before her, he dipped down and placed an arm under her ass and lifted her until she sat on the marble countertop.

Firmly wedged between her open thighs, Baran reached behind her and undid the clasp of her bra, letting it fall to the floor. Lerna moaned as Baran gripped the back of her neck. His gold eyes locked onto hers, and she could see the desire and need in his gaze. She reached up, running her fingers through his hair, pulling his face down to meet hers. Their lips met in a passionate kiss, their tongues tangling together, wringing out every bit of emotion in that simple connection.

Baran broke the kiss and whispered a soft, "I need you," in her ear. Lerna trembled at the intense hunger he revealed. He grasped her hips and pulled her to the edge of the counter until she hovered over the hardened length of his cock.

With a deep thrust, she sheathed him fully, gasping at the sensation of being utterly filled by him. Baran's hands gripped her hips, holding her steady as he took her hard and fast.

Lerna wrapped her legs around Baran's waist, her head falling back with every powerful thrust.

Baran's breath came in ragged gasps as he drove into her harder, his hips demanding, his heart pounding against his ribs. Lerna's moans filled the air, a symphony of passion and desire that echoed off the bathroom walls. Her nails dug into his back, pulling him closer, deeper, harder.

Sweat glistened on their skin as they moved, the sounds of their lovemaking growing more frantic, more intense. Lerna arched her back, her orgasm building within her, a fiery inferno that threatened to consume her whole. He pounded into her harder, his cock swelling within her, the sensation of her warmth surrounding him, driving him on.

Lerna's orgasm hit her like a freight train, her world shattering as wave after wave of pleasure washed over her. Her screams filled the room. Baran felt the familiar pressure building within him, the knowledge that he was seconds away from his own release.

With one final, powerful thrust, Baran came, his seed filling her, his yell joining hers in the cacophony of passion. They collapsed onto the cool marble, their bodies still joined, their hearts pounding in unison.

As they caught their breath, Baran pulled out of her, his cock leaving a wet trail between her legs. He wrapped his arms around her, pulling her close. Lifting her into his arms, he stepped into the warm water in the tub. She murmured sleepily as he lowered them, thanking his mother for her insistence on remodeling the bathroom and including the soaking tub.

Contentment flooded Baran as he took care of his mate,

gently washing her body as she relaxed against him. By the time he was done and dried her off, she was asleep on her feet. He lowered her to the bed and climbed in behind her, holding her close as he drifted off to sleep.

CHAPTER 21

A sound drew Lerna from her slumber. Soft light flooded the room through the sheer shades. She ran her hand over where Baran had been sleeping next to her, but a cold, empty space was all she found. At the end of the bed, a dark blue blanket draped across her feet. As she threw back the covers, she shivered in the cool morning air. The cold front that Jasper said was coming seemed to have hit overnight.

Wrapping the blanket around her shoulders, she moved to the window and discovered what had woken her. Down below, Baran stood at a large stump in the ground with an axe buried in the top. His warm breath puffed out in a cloud into the cold air. He unbuttoned the red and black buffalo plaid flannel he wore, stripping it off his muscular arms to reveal a tight, white tank top underneath. As Lerna watched, he continued working, the muscles flexing and contracting in his arms and back as he lifted the axe. Baran's muscles glistened with sweat with each swing of the axe. The smooth, rhythmic motion of his arm, the powerful force behind each blow, and the determination on his face made her heart race. As Baran took another swing, pieces of wood flew off and landed on the frozen ground with a thud. It made him pause for a moment; the sound echoing in the quiet morning air. He picked up the pieces and placed them on a large stack. He looked up at the window where she stood and caught her watching him. She reached out her hand and placed her palm on the glass. Baran swung the axe and buried it back into the stump, and picked up his shirt.

A knock at the door drew her attention away from him.

"Come in," Lerna said, clutching the blanket tighter.

Holly peeked her head in and saw her up out of the bed.

"Good morning. I brought your other bag up."

She lifted the canvas bag with her recent purchases.

"I hope you bought a jacket. It's gotten chilly out."

"Baran made sure I did."

"Breakfast is almost ready if you're hungry. You've probably worked up quite an appetite," she said.

Lerna's face flushed hot. Of course, they knew what she and Baran had been up to last night with their super hearing and all.

"I'm sorry," Holly blurted. "I didn't mean to embarrass you."

"You didn't. I'm not used to talking about stuff so openly."

"Sex is a natural part of life. I'd be worried if you two weren't burning up the sheets. Get dressed and come down before the food gets cold, okay?"

"I'll be there in a minute."

Lerna descended the stairs, hearing conversation coming from below. As her foot touched the third step, Baran appeared at the bottom. He now sported a navy blue t-shirt and his hair was damp and disheveled, as though he had run his hand through it. When his eyes landed on her, he pounded up the stairs, wrapping his arms around her waist and drawing her close to him.

"Morning," he murmured, pressing his lips against hers. "Sleep well?"

"I did," she replied with a smile.

"She should have been worn out from all the moaning and screaming coming from the room," Vonn quipped from the other room.

Lerna buried her face in Baran's chest in embarrassment.

"Shut up, you asshole. That's my mate you're talking about," Baran snarled.

"Sorry, Lerna. I didn't mean to hurt your feelings. I'm just teasing you. Isn't that what you're supposed to do with a little sister?" asked Vonn, coming around the corner and looking up at them.

"Vonn, take your ass outside and check the perimeter. I don't want to be caught unaware if those assholes show up."

"You got it, boss." Vonn gave a two-finger salute and waltzed out the way he came.

"Come on, babe. Let's get you some breakfast. I'm sure you're hungry," Baran raised his eyebrows playfully and Lerna couldn't help but laugh.

"You're just as bad as he is."

"The difference is I can get away with it because you're my mate."

Every time he called her his mate, a sense of rottenness settled and burned into her soul. How could that be possible? She was human, and he was a shifter.

"Lead the way, mate," she said, and he growled in response as his eyes flashed gold.

"I like it when you call me that." His hand cupped the side of her neck, thumb stroking the soft skin. "Food first," he whispered.

"Then what?"

"Then I take you back to bed." He leaned in when his lips were a hairsbreadth away from hers. He whispered, "We didn't break it in enough last night."

"Promises, promises," she replied in a husky voice.

Her stomach chose that moment to growl, breaking the mood. He gave her a quick kiss before throwing her over his shoulder in a fireman's carry and swatting her on the ass.

"Food, woman."

CHAPTER 22

Lerna spent most of the day sitting on the front porch wrapped in a fuzzy blanket, reading on her e-reader while Baran did chores around the cabin. When she offered to help, he told her to rest and relax. Overall, it wasn't bad since she got to ogle Baran as he worked without his shirt on. Sweat glistened on his skin as he continued to add to the growing pile of firewood.

Holly and Vonn had disappeared after breakfast, but she had seen a flash of tawny hair in between the numerous trees lining the property once or twice. Deciding she needed to do something helpful, Lerna headed indoors to find something to make for lunch. Since the refrigerator was full, she pulled out the fixings to make sandwiches. Lerna debated on how much to fix, but decided three might fill up Baran. She'd watched him put away more food than any man she'd ever seen before. Placing them on a plate, she also added chips, a sliced apple, and a few chocolate chip cookies.

When she reappeared on the porch with her hands full, Baran's head whipped around in her direction. He buried the axe and grabbed his shirt, and he hurried over to her.

"I made us some lunch. I know it's not much-"

"It's perfect. Thank you." He leaned over and kissed her. "I'm starving."

"I forgot the drinks. Here," she said, handing him the plates. "Be right back."

She went back in and grabbed the two glasses of iced sweet tea she had left on the counter. Outside, Baran had taken a seat on the wide, wooden steps, the plates placed beside him.

"Here you go," she said, handing him the glass and sitting down beside him.

"You didn't have to go to all this trouble, but I appreciate it."

"You've been working hard out here. I knew you had to be getting hungry."

Sunlight dappled the yard through the trees as various creatures made sounds. Baran was on his second sandwich when a weird chirping sound filled the air. He paused mid chew and looked out at the tree line separating the yard from the natural terrain. He placed the sandwich down and stood on alert.

"Go in the house," he ordered.

"What?" Lerna asked, confused. "What's going on?"

"In the house, now," he barked out. "They're here."

"Oh shit," she hissed out. "Come with me," she begged, grabbing his arm.

"It's okay, Lerna. We have this planned out. It'll all be over soon. Go upstairs, close the curtains and stay away from the windows." He turned and gave her a soft kiss. "Please. I need to know you're safe."

Lerna's gaze roved over his face, fear creeping up her spine. What if she lost him? In a short amount of time, he meant so much to her.

"You stay safe," she uttered. "All of you. I'll never forgive myself if something happened to you."

"We'll be fine and once this is over, we can start our lives together."

She stepped into his arms and melted against him as he pulled her to his chest.

"I love you," she whispered, holding back the tears that threatened to spill.

"I love you too, my mate."

He looked down at her before kissing her.

"Now please, go inside and stay there."

With reluctance, she let him go and went inside, locking the door behind her. Upstairs, she pulled the curtains closed after watching Baran return to the pile of wood and stacking the pieces he had left on the ground. As she sat on the edge of the bed, she heard tires crunching on the gravel.

Her heart pounded as one door closed, then another. Enzo and Angelo had arrived.

CHAPTER 23

Baran watched out of the corner of his eye as the black SUV crawled down the driveway. Two dark-haired men sat in the front. He placed the two pieces of wood on the stack and turned to face them as they exited the vehicle. The driver was tall, with a shaved head and built like a bull. His dark gray suit stretched across his massive shoulders, but did little to hide the gun he had on his side. He kept his face expressionless as he stared at Baran from behind dark glasses. He moved around the front of the vehicle, opening the door for the passenger.

Baran knew this was Angelo the second he stepped out. Even to Baran's untrained eye, he could tell the suit he wore was expensive, along with his loafers. Angelo smiled when he looked at Baran as if he thought he had the upper hand. In his eyes, he probably did, seeing as they were armed and outnumbered him. Little did they know. Baran bit back the smile that threatened to break free.

"Can I help you?"

"I think you can," Angelo answered, taking off his sunglasses and tucking them in the breast pocket of his jacket. "I'm looking for a woman."

"Aren't we all?"

"I believe that you've met her. Lerna Porter?"

"What makes you think I know her?"

"Word is you found a woman in the middle of the road and helped her."

"Oh her? I dropped her off at the bus station." Baran shrugged. "Gave her some cash for a ticket and left her there."

Angelo shook his head. "Why don't I believe that, Mr. Rhodes?"

Baran's eyes shot wide as if surprised Angelo knew who he was.

"I know all about you, Mr. Rhodes. And you took my girl home to your raggedly little trailer. Where is she now, Rhodes? I want her back."

Baran's cat scratched at his insides, begging to be let out so he could rip out the man's throat for talking about their mate. She was theirs, dammit.

"Sorry. Don't have a clue."

"She's in the house, isn't she?" Angelo shook his head with a laugh. "Does she think that will protect her?"

"It's time for you to leave," Baran said, clenching his fists tight.

"Lerna, it's time to come out and play," Angelo yelled at the house tauntingly.

With his human hearing, Angelo couldn't hear the whimper that she emitted, but Baran did, and it infuriated him. His mate should never feel fear with him there to protect her.

"Leave now," Baran ground out, taking a step toward Angelo.

Enzo whipped out his gun and aimed it at him. Baran feigned fear and stopped short of reaching Angelo.

"Lerna, I know you can hear me. Come out now before lover boy gets hurt."

"She's not in there."

"I'm going to count to three, and if you're not standing in front of me, Lerna, he's going to pay the price. Is that what you want?" Angelo yelled at the house.

Baran prayed Lerna listened to him and stayed put.

"One, two, three. Enzo," Angelo said, nodding at the man.

The retort of the gun was loud, and pain seared Baran's shoulder. He reached up and wrapped his hand around the wound. He could see his brother creeping up beside the SUV in his cat form.

"No!" Lerna screamed from inside the cabin.

Her footsteps pounded as she ran down the stairs inside. Baran closed his eyes and cursed.

"Lerna, stay inside!" Baran ordered.

He heard her stopped short of the front door. Her heart was pounding, and the scent of her fear permeated the air.

Angelo pulled a gun from his waistband and pointed it at Baran's head.

"The next one will end him, Lerna. I'm not playing with you anymore. Come out here and I may let him live."

Baran sensed the rest of his pride gathering closer to the men. They only needed a little more time. He readied himself to pounce when the knob on the front door turned.

"No, don't hurt him," Lerna cried as she stepped onto the porch.

"Go back inside, Lerna."

"I can't let him hurt you because of me," she sobbed.

"Do you trust me?" Baran asked, not taking his eyes off Angelo.

"Yes."

"Touching," Angelo mocked. "Lerna, I will put a bullet in his head if you don't come down here."

When she didn't move, Angelo pushed the gun to Baran's forehead.

Lerna hesitated. She trusted Baran, but what if he was

wrong? Yes, shifters were resilient, but could he survive a bullet to the brain?

"Now, Lerna," Angelo ordered.

She knew he would do it; had seen him do it before.

"Promise you'll leave him alone," Lerna bargained.

"You're in no position to be asking me favors."

"Please, Angelo," she begged.

Angelo lowered the gun and looked at her, as did Baran. Tears streaked her cheeks, and she clenched the hem of her shirt in her fists. Baran inclined his head, giving Vonn the signal, and rushed Angelo. He must have caught the movement out of the corner of his eye as he fired, hitting Baran in the chest, causing him to fall backward. It hurt like a son of a bitch, but Baran knew it wasn't fatal. Lerna, on the other hand, didn't.

She screamed as he hit the ground and rushed off the porch toward him.

"Baran," she cried out as she ran to him.

Enzo's scream of agony drew her up short as she looked on in horror. Baran looked over to see Vonn pinning Enzo to the ground with his claws digging deep into his chest before he clamped his mouth around Enzo's neck, biting down. Blood streamed on the ground as Vonn raised his head with part of Enzo's throat in his mouth.

Baran couldn't stop the smile of satisfaction from his face as he rose from the ground to face Angelo, only to realize he was no longer in front of him. He was now behind Lerna, holding the gun to her head.

"Let her go," Baran growled.

"What the fuck are you? How did you…"

"I said let her go," Baran's voice became rougher as his cat fought to be free. He wanted his vengeance for the man putting his hands on their mate.

"Bbbbaran?" Lerna's voice quivered as she looked at him.

Golden hairs peppered his arms and his claws protruded

from his fingertips. Lerna had seen him shift into his cat, but not like this. Half man, half cat.

"Stay back, you freak, or I'll kill her," Angelo threatened.

"If you hurt a hair on her head, you'll die in agony. Let her go and I'll make it quick," Baran promised. "Either way, you're not leaving here alive."

"The bitch is mine," Angelo screamed. Lerna flinched and closed her eyes.

Baran saw a blur of silvery gray fur on the roof. Holly crept down toward the edge of the roof behind Angelo. She looked at him with wide eyes as she readied to pounce.

"Lerna, look at me."

Her brown eyes locked with his.

"It's going to be okay. Now drop."

Her eyes widened before she let herself fall to the ground. Angelo lost his grip on Lerna as Holly leapt from the roof and landed on his back.

Angelo screamed as she dug in her claws. He dropped the gun, trying to reach the lynx clinging to his back. Lerna moved out of the way as Baran completed his shift into his cat.

Holly dropped from Angelo's back as Baran charged toward him, hitting him full force. Angelo landed on his back, pinned to the ground as Baran dug his claws into his chest. The smell of piss infiltrated his nose, and he sneezed at the pungent aroma. Baran pulled his cat back until only his claws remained. He dug them deeper into Angelo's skin until he hit bone.

Baran leaned down until his face was mere inches from Angelo's.

"You touched my mate, hunted her, scared her. If not for you, I may never have met her and I thank you for that. But for the same reasons, you need to die."

Baran reared back and slashed his claws across the soft skin of Angelo's throat. Bright red blood wept from the gouges left by his claws. Angelo lifted his hands to his neck, trying to stem the flow, but it puddled underneath him until the light left his eyes. Baran watched and listened until his heart beat for the last time. He stood from his kill and looked at Lerna. Holly had positioned herself in front of her, pacing back and forth.

"Bro," Vonn called, tossing Baran a pair of shorts. "Cover it up, man."

He pulled the black shorts on and walked toward Lerna. She stared at him with wide eyes. He could only imagine the way he looked to her. Blood covered his torso and hands. Hesitating, he stopped, afraid she now saw him as a monster.

"Are you all right? Are you hurt?"

She shook her head.

"I'm fine. You're the one who was shot. Twice."

Baran glanced at the healed wounds on his shoulder and chest.

"They're already healed."

"Really?"

"Yes. I told you we're-"

She launched herself at him, cutting his words short. He caught her in his arms as she wrapped herself around him and buried her head in his neck. Her body shook as she sobbed against him.

"Shh, it's okay. We're fine. All of us."

"I was so scared. When he put that gun to your head, I thought that I was going to lose you."

"I'd never let that happen. Not when I've just found you."

CHAPTER 24

Later that night, the pride said goodnight as they headed back to the RV park, leaving Baran and Lerna alone for the first time. Lerna didn't understand why she was nervous to be alone with him, but she'd been on edge ever since Holly and Vonn had left.

"Are you hungry?" Baran asked as he came up behind her.

"Not really," she answered.

"Is something bothering you?"

"I-"

"If it's about today, I'm sorry you saw that side of me," Baran uttered dejectedly.

Lerna turned in his arms.

"What are you talking about?"

"The monster."

"You're not a monster, Baran, and that thought never once crossed my mind."

"Are you sure?" His gaze searched her face.

"Yes. I'm nervous about tonight."

"Why tonight?"

"I want to become your mate."

His hands came up, framing her face.

"Truly?"

"Yes. I want to be your mate and stay here with you. I have it on good authority that someone doesn't like doing the books."

Before she realized it, he laid her over his shoulder as he sprinted up the stairs and into the bedroom. Her back hit the mattress with a bounce as she laughed.

"Baran, what in the world?"

"I'm not waiting a second longer to make you mine," he growled, pulling off his boots.

She reached for the hem of her shirt, but he stopped her.

"Stop. That's my job."

Her breath quickened as her panties dampened. Baran's touch was electrifying as he slid her shirt up and over her head, his eyes never leaving hers. Lerna could feel the tension building between them, the desire palpable in the air. Their lips met in a fiery kiss, igniting a passion that had been simmering beneath the surface all day long. Baran's hands roamed her body as he removed her clothes, sending shivers down her spine as he traced every curve and dip with reverence. Lerna melted into his touch, giving herself over to the moment.

"Could you be any more perfect?" he murmured against her skin.

"Baran, please," she pleaded, needing more of him.

He grinned as he stood up. He pulled his shirt over his head. Lerna's gaze traced each delineated muscled on his arms and chest as she licked her lips. His hands moved to the button of his jeans and he heard her whimper. Baran chuckled at her reaction, the sound deep and husky. He peeled off his jeans, revealing the powerful muscles of his thighs and the tantalizing outline of his hardened length straining against his boxer briefs. Lerna felt a rush of heat pooling between her thighs as she hungrily took in his powerful body, knowing that it belonged to her. He shoved the boxer briefs down, freeing his hardened shaft. He gripped his cock in his hand and stroked it a few times. Unable to hold back, he crawled over her like the predator he was, his hands caressing her skin, igniting a trail of fire wherever they touched. His lips skimmed her soft skin until he reached her breast. Engulfing her nipple in his mouth, he sucked until she writhed beneath him with hungry cries for more.

He moved down her stomach, teasing her with his hot breath before reaching her fiery core. Baran parted her lips, letting his tongue flick over her aching clit. She cried out, her hips bucking up to meet his touch. The sensation was intense, but not enough. She craved something deeper.

Baran, knowing what they needed, stood up. He pulled her to the edge of the bed and flipped her over until she was on her hands and knees, ass in the air, her needy pussy open and ready for him. She felt him line up at her entrance, his powerful cock pressing against her sensitive flesh. Lerna whimpered, waiting for the moment she'd been dreaming of all day.

With a single forceful thrust, he slammed into her, filling her completely. She cried out, her body trembling from the impact. Baran clamped a hand on her hip and one on her shoulder to keep her in place as he drove into her. Each thrust drove them to the edge. Lerna's cries filled the air. Baran moved his hand from her hip to splay across her lower stomach until his finger could rub against her clit. Her pussy fluttered around him as she screamed out her release. He leaned down and bit into the curve of her neck, infusing her with his essence. She jerked against him as pleasure overrode any pain she may have felt. Her sheath milked his cock, dragging his release from his body.

His knees felt weak as he emptied himself into her, marking her for all time as his mate. As he released her neck, he licked the wounds, sealing them up with his saliva. He rested his forehead in the middle of her back as he fought to catch his breath. Picking her up, he placed her in the middle of the bed and curled himself around her.

"How do you feel, mate?"

"Perfect," she near purred, eyes full of love.

A smile tugged at the corner of her lips as she cuddled into his embrace.

"Better than perfect," she corrected, nuzzling her nose against his warm chest. "I've never felt more complete."

Baran's grip tightened around her, pulling her closer until her head rested on his shoulder.

"I couldn't have said it better myself."

ALSO BY SAMANTHA CONLEY

Silver Tongued Devils Series

Down in Flames

Break Me Down

Down on My Knees

Crashing Down

Silver Tongued Devil's Boxset

Whiskey Bend Series

Pieces of a Broken Heart

Beat of My Heart

ALSO BY SAMANTHA CONLEY

ABOUT THE AUTHOR

Samantha is a multifaceted individual, balancing the roles of a devoted wife, nurturing mother, and compassionate Registered Nurse. Beyond her professional and family commitments, she shares a deep passion for the world of romance novels. When not tending to patients or spending quality time with her loved ones, you'll likely find her engrossed in the pages of a captivating romance book. And, just between us, she's been known to sneak in some reading during work hours, though she hopes her boss never finds out!

Her household is a bustling haven filled with the warmth of family and the presence of adorable fur babies who bring joy and chaos in equal measure. In her moments of relaxation and inspiration, she dedicates her time to crafting enchanting love stories that transport readers to worlds of passion, emotion, and romance.

One of her little secrets? An addiction to Dr. Pepper Zero and a penchant for sweet and spicy pickles, providing a delightful combination of flavors that fuel her creativity and satisfy her cravings.

www.samanthaconleyauthor.com
www.facebook.com/authorsconley/
www.facebook.com/groups/SamanthaConleysReaders/
www.instagram.com/author_samantha_conley/
www.bookbub.com/authorsamanthaconley/